SPECIAL LOVE

BLAZIN' LOVE BOOK FIVE

JA'NESE DIXON

PUBLISHING

CONTENTS

SNEAK PEEK: ROCKSTAR SECRETS

What will it take to win his heart...again?

It's Freedom Day.

I couldn't see myself married until I conquered my career. So, when Maximus dropped to one knee in front of our family and friends, I freaked.

I'm Parker Hamilton. I should be experiencing an all-time high, as a partner of Platinum Prestige and a top real estate agent in Texas. But I don't have my man, and it's lonelier than I imagined.

So, I decided to host a soiree on a party bus taking my guests through Austin Hill Country, I don't expect to see Max board, especially with her.

She's the woman I've hated since she took kiddie

scissors to my ponytail. The one who "accidentally" dropped fruit punch on my cream prom dress. The woman that finds a way to sabotage every picture perfect moment.

When Max looks at me, I can still see the hunger in his eyes.

Ready or not, I have four hours to make him mine again. And this time, I'm willing to do whatever it takes to get a second chance.

CHAPTER 1

PARKER

"'m about to bring the party to you," I scream, opening the charter bus door. Today is all about my guys and not about me trying to fight the hollowness lurking inside me. I hope hanging with my besties and the potential to make a hefty commission is a perfect remedy to tackle the downward spiral of my internal debates. "I hope you paid your babysitters well because we're not returning until after bedtime."

The herd runs in my direction as I step outside the fifty-six-passenger bus. "Charlee stop pushing."

"I'm childfree, and I got my man to myself…you better mind your business." She bumps me with her hip, and I buckle over to hear her laugh.

"Well, get your child-free butt on the bus crazy lady." I hug her husband, Darius, smiling as they disappear onto the bus.

This is the first stop. I organized a multi-million-dollar home tour in the Austin Hill Country to celebrate the holidays. My guys, business partners, and best friends load the bus to help and relax for the day. They each are assigned a station on the tour.

Hunter and Ben board, followed by Harper and Liam. I shield my eyes from the sun as I watch Taylor and Zach head my way.

"How's the remodeling going?"

Zach gives me a strong brotherly hug. "Ask my wife."

"Oh brother, what happened Taylor?" Her hair is styled in some cinnamon brown faux dreadlocks, her new style of choice.

"I'm tired of having my house filled with workers and all of the dust. I'm ready for them to be done already." She kisses my cheek.

"The addition of an art studio will increase the value on your home."

"Yeah, yeah, yeah. I just want Zach to have a place to create." Taylor looks over at him, and I wish I could patent the look in her eyes. "So, if they have to keep hammering to make it happen...baby, please tell me this won't take forever."

"It won't take forever, love." Zach leans in to kiss her, and I turn away.

"Promise?" The whine in her voice causes him to chuckle.

"Promise." Zach says with such assurance that I stop

to admire them. They fought for love and won. I had that once.

"All right love birds. Keep moving." I tease as they board with the rest of the guys.

The final guys, Chase, Jordan, Payton, Alex, and Ryann, pull up the rear. I climb the stairs signaling for the bus driver to close the door behind me. The charter rolls into motion, and I take the microphone.

"Welcome! I'm Parker Belle Hamilton your tour guide and trusted real estate agent."

Thunderous clapping fills the bus as if they don't know what I do. These women and their husbands are my family. We do life together. They're the vertebrae to my spine. I can't do life without them.

"Quiet down. We have a full day ahead. So, welcome to my Freedom Day slash 4th of July celebration. Thank you to my guys and your wonderful husbands for blocking out this day to assist me. We're expecting forty tourists, and we'll visit ten houses."

"Are all of the houses still on the market?" I glance toward Liam, Harper's husband, a few rows back.

"Yes, all of the houses are available. I'll gladly submit offers on your behalf if needed."

The group laughs. They each contribute to the success of my real estate business. Several of them have bought homes from me. I'm even working on a construction project with Taylor and Zach, on rental properties.

"These are upper tier clients. I've included all of your

business details in the folders. But don't forget, in the words of the infamous Charlee Grant, 'Y'all heifers better have some fun!'" I snap my finger and roll my neck.

"Ha ha ha." Charlee's sarcasm sends the guys into a fit of laughter again.

I pick back up. "We have a few minutes to settle in and get ready. Spread out and mingle. You guys are my eyes and ears."

"Don't worry. We got you covered." Alex leans forwards and squeezes my hand.

"I know that's why I love you guys." It warms my heart.

"Don't you start that sappy stuff." Charlee yells from the back.

"Hush! Okay. Let me get ready."

I turn off the microphone and lower to the front seat. They have other places they should be and businesses they run outside of Platinum Prestige, our elite concierge service Hunter started three years ago. The ten of us—Hunter, Harper, Charlee, Taylor, Chase, Jordan, Payton, Alex, Ryann and I—are equal partners and as they each marry off and start their lives, their husbands, Ben, Liam, Darius, and Zach have rallied around us. It's the oddest, realest, happiest time in my life. And it's *almost* perfect.

Seeing my guys happy and in love makes me wonder if I let my ambition fuel a colossal mistake. The mistake of choosing my career over my relationship. The rate of my heart slows and the ache I try to hide rears its head.

There's no point in revisiting the ghost of my past. I

shake off the thought. Today is a big day for me and Parker Belle Realty.

"Ready to review the checklist?" Chase Elliott moves up to the seat behind me. She's my right-hand today, not because she works in real estate but because she organizes showcases and hosts parties for her artists.

I open my iPad, and we run through the day. She heads back to her seat while I review the specs of each of the houses on the tour—the square footage, amenities, neighborhood features, all the details that make a house a home.

I sell multi-million-dollar homes as one of the top real estate agents in the state of Texas. The bulk of my homes are in Austin, Houston, and the Dallas/Fort Worth area. The fact that I'm a month past my thirtieth birthday is evidence of how hard I've hustled to build my career.

The bus rolls to a stop outside Smith & Jameson International Beer Garden. It is essentially our hub until we voted to start looking for an official office for Platinum Prestige, which is at the top of my list after I get through this tour. We leased a space, but the location felt stale.

"Charlee, are you ready?" I call over my shoulder, scanning the group gathered in the parking lot. The nervous energy in my body is pulsing because it's almost showtime.

"I got you boo."

The guys stand in unison rocking their Parker Belle

shirts. Charlee kisses Darius and moves forward to take the microphone. She's the mistress of ceremony for the tour.

"I'm jumping off to run to the restroom and gather my thoughts." I inform them as I drop my phone in my back pocket.

"You got fifteen minutes." Chase says, and I nod checking the time.

The doors open and I sweep past the crowd as they move toward the bus. Each of the passengers paid for a ticket to join us today. I can trust my guys to collect tickets, get the people situated, and keep them entertained.

I handle my business then I stop to speak with Jazz, one of the owners. This is our first and last stop.

"You guys can join us. We have room for you." I offer before confirming the VIP room set up and food.

"The last thing I need is Asher buying another house." She chuckles, dropping her head. "But the way we keep having these kids, I might need to change my mind."

I laugh. "Think about what you need and your budget. I can put together a private showing for you."

"I'll do that."

I hear the chime of my phone in my back pocket. "I bet that's Chase. I gotta go. I can't be late for my own tour." We hug. "I'll see you around Happy Hour."

"We'll be here."

I head out to the bus, taking a moment to check my reflection in the mirrors behind the bar. I wave to

Martinez, the regular bartender. Then I fluff my bun and run a finger over my gloss. I opted for my cat-eye glasses and a tailored suit over my Parker Belle tee. I'm sure I'll regret wearing these heels, but they complete my outfit.

I proudly embrace my youth and professionalism in everything I do. My phone chimes again and I pick up my pace walking to the bus. I reach for my phone when I stop dead in my tracks. The guys are in a huddle outside the bus. They turn in my direction as if sensing my presence.

"What's going on?" I glance at my phone, seeing I have two new messages from Chase. I scan their faces. "What is it?"

Charlee opens her mouth to respond when Harper grips her forearm. Harper is the peacemaker in our group. She's the one called on to deliver sad news, bad news, difficult news. She handles conflict with ease, except for once, when she met her husband, Liam. That put her in rare form.

"We haven't even made it to the first stop, and Harper is up." I chuckle trying to relieve the tension.

"This is taking too long."

"Charlee." They say in unison.

"Stephanie boarded shortly after you left." Harper steps forward, and the guys block my view of the bus.

"Stephanie? Stephanie, who?" It can't be who I think it is. I haven't seen her in years.

"Stephanie Towns." Chase confirms.

This chick cut my ponytail in elementary school.

Stephanie "accidentally" spilled fruit punch down my cream prom dress. She managed to pop up at every memorable school event until we graduated from high school, and she's here now.

"I'm over it. That's years ago. This is about money, and I have houses to sell." I try to sidestep Harper, and Hunter stops me.

"That's not it. She came with Max."

"My Max." I step back, my throat suddenly dry.

They nod, and I can't look at their faces. I drop my head to gather my thoughts. I've planned this tour for months, and I haven't seen Max in eight long years. But no matter how long its been, I still love him.

"Does he know this is my tour?"

Harper wraps an arm around me. "He didn't say anything. But he'd have to be deaf, dumb, and blind not to know."

"To his credit, he looked surprised when he saw me." Chase adds. "So, what's the verdict? We need to get this bus moving."

"Let's get this party started." I say the words, but I can't deny I'm worried about what I'll do when I come face to face with Max.

"Ah, *shyte*! That's my girl." Charlee hoots.

They head to the entrance of the bus. I'm pulling up the rear, Charlee stops before we board.

"Let me know if you need a moment." I nod. This one is the life of the party but soft and sweet on the inside.

"Seeing an ex is hard when you have unfinished business."

"I'm good. That was eight years ago."

Her eyes hold a hint of disbelief. "The offer stands. And if you need somebody to throw some bows... I'm your guy."

I throw my head back and laugh until I brush away the tears. "I love your crazy butt."

"And you should."

I accept her embrace, then Charlee climbs the stairs. I pause for a moment. Eight years were a lifetime ago and at that time Maximus Bradley it. He was everything I'd ever wanted in a man until.... *Stop Parker. I'm over this.*

I climb the stairs, I pat Denzel, the driver on the back, before turning to my guests. Then my eyes lock with *his*.

CHAPTER 2

MAX

I've never not wanted to be in a place more than right now. The bus moves, music plays, the conversations flow. But I'm trapped between a conniving woman and the woman who changed my life *forever*.

"Max," Stephanie leans into my side.

I hold up a hand. I don't trust myself, not right now. My emotions are unpredictable when I'm breathing the same air as Parker Belle Hamilton.

She's standing less than five feet away. I haven't seen her in eight years, and now here they are, seeing each other again, like this.

I start at the top of her messy blonde bun with stray curls fighting to break free. The stylish glasses are paired with delicate pearl earrings. Her suit fits like a second skin, and my manhood swells with each passing second.

Parker is the silent threat I never saw coming, and she wears time well. How did she get more beautiful?

"How long is this tour?" I ask, unable to pull my eyes from Parker.

"Four hours."

"Four hours!" My head jerks to Stephanie. Her face is unreadable. "Why exactly did you select *this* tour? Because it's Parker's tour?" I say her name and my nerves tingle. I can't believe she still does this to me.

"No. I heard about the houses included in the tour. Most of them are exclusive listings through Parker Belle Realty. I know one of them will satisfy your requirements. And—"

I lift a hand, silencing her again. My gut told me not to believe Stephanie. She and Parker have been enemies for as long as I can remember, now I look like a traitor.

What Parker and I shared happened long ago, but I'd never do anything to hurt her or cause her harm intentionally. I rub the back of my neck, stacking the facts like Legos.

"Max, I'm over that high school bull. This is about helping your company expand in this market."

Stephanie Towns came highly recommended. I reached out to her since we grew up in the same schools in the same neighborhood. I plan to spend a small fortune to make this transition happen. I figured I might as well invest in the business of an acquaintance. But seeing the look in Parker's eyes have me second guessing my decision.

"I hope you're right. Because this shit looks messy and I don't run my business like this."

I glance back in Parker's direction. She's sitting in the front seat. I stand focused on her trying to feel past the heat churning in my body. I take two steps, and my path is blocked.

"Ryann, Alex, it's been a while."

"It has. But not that long." Ryann throws her eyes towards Stephanie.

I follow her gaze. I can remind them that this is a business. But I know Parker's guys well enough to avoid a situation.

"I didn't know this was Parker's tour. I'm heading to clear the air." I extend an arm in Parker's direction, not quite sure what I'll say.

"Max," Ryann steps forward as Alex retakes her seat. "This is important to her."

"And?"

I lock eyes with Ryann. She is taller than an average woman. We stand eye-to-eye, and I'm reminded of how they roll. The guys became a formidable clique in high school. Their unit is tighter than the Secret Service. One for all and ten for one.

"And..." A slow smile crosses her face, I wouldn't consider it friendly, but a matter of fact. "We're surrounded by some of Austin's top business owners, political officials, and artists. Whatever personal matters you have with Parker should take place privately."

I glance around the bus, letting my eyes linger longer

this time. I recognize many of the faces. I weigh my options.

"Thanks for the advice."

I walk past her to the front of the bus. I unbutton my suit jacket surveying the area. All the seats around her are occupied except the one beside her.

"Parker."

"Max." Her eyes are sharp and assessing. The thin smile tells the truth of her feelings.

"Got a second?"

She slides over until her back is against the window. I lower into the seat beside her. I sit back, watching the city through the wide windshield. Then I glance over my shoulder at her.

God, she's beautiful.

"How—" We say in unison.

She laughs, fiddling with her glasses. "Go ahead."

"How are you, Parker?"

"I 'm…good. Better than good, really. How about you? How are you?"

"Life keeps me moving at a faster than normal pace. But I'm living my dream. So, I won't complain."

"Are you still in—"

"New York. Yes, that's home now." I pull away from her eyes to bring my emotions under control. "And is this all you?" I lift a hand to the bus, the people.

"Sort of. I'm still in real estate plus rental property and a business with the guys."

"Doing it big. You always said you'd make your first million before your thirtieth birthday."

"And I did."

"Nothing and no one stands in Parker Belle Hamilton's way." Her nose flares. The words slipped out really, but now they hang between us like a brick anchored to our past, and suddenly we're sinking.

"Is there a reason you're here, Max?"

"In Austin or on your bus?"

"Both." Her arms cross as if holding herself back.

"I was invited."

"By Stephanie?" I nod.

Parker turns, facing ahead with stiff dignity. I let my eyes caress her profile. I want to touch her, but that's out of the question. Parker is the type of woman every man wants until he learns she won't hesitate to put her dreams and aspirations before anything and anyone, even love.

"Well, I hope you enjoy the activities we have planned for the day." The fake chipper tone grinds my nerves like worn brakes.

"That's fucked up Parker."

"Ditto, Max." Her head snaps towards me, her face clouded in anger. "We have several guides available in a lemon colored Parker Belle tees. I'm available if they're unable to answer your questions."

"It's like that?" I stand up. Trying to talk with her is a bad idea.

"I don't know, you tell me. Oh, and send Stephanie my best."

"Fine."

I WALK BACK to my seat. This is bullshit, and she knows it. I see Ryann, and her stern expression doesn't help. We're thirty minutes into this tour, and I'm an Uber away from returning to my hotel. I fold over the knot in my stomach.

"Max."

I glance over at Stephanie, the woman responsible for making today possible. But she appears to be cut from ice.

"Max."

I look left and right, and I see a pair of eyes between the seat. Then a gift bag slips through the small opening. Darius Chocolates is etched in gold foil outside the black paper bag.

"Do me a favor?" Charlee sits up, resting on the top of the head rest. "Enjoy the chocolate, and the day we have planned." She looks over her shoulder to the front and back at me.

"Charlee Raine…" I hear the voice but can't see the man through the crack of the seats.

"My husband, Darius. Darius, do you remember Max?"

"Hey, man. You good?" He glances around the edge of the seat and Charlee lowers back into the seat.

"I was until I wasn't."

Darius' boisterous laugh overpowers the music. I can't help but join him.

"The guys have that effect on most men. Sit back and holler at me once we stop at the first house. I'll introduce you to the fellas."

"I'd like that."

"I got you."

We shake hands, and Darius disappears back around the seat. I open the bag and bite into the chocolate.

"That's good." I whisper beneath my breath.

"Damn right."

Charlee is still Charlee. I take Darius' advice and recline in the chair. I allow my teeth to sink into the morsel thinking about Parker.

I thought Parker was the one. So much so that I knelt on one knee in front of our family and friends and asked for her hand in marriage. The happiest day of my life became the worse day of my life. Because the love of my life said, "No."

I pop the last piece in my mouth. I need a house, and expanding my company into Texas is important to me.

The pushback from the current legislation in my home state has me joining forces with a lobbying firm to help further the laws concerning how food and beverage delivery companies function in the state. Which means I've committed to flying back and forth between New York and Austin to make this happen.

I'll partake of today's tour focused on my goal, and

not Parker, subjecting myself to her again is grounds for undoing all I've managed to build. I inhale deeply and exhale slowly to calm my racing heart. And I'm not having that. I can't let her in again.

I *overreacted.* I fold over in the seat yanking off my glasses, squeezing the bridge of my nose.

"Miss Hamilton?"

"Yes, Denzel." I met the bus driver's eyes in the rearview mirror.

"You have less than fifteen minutes."

"Thank you."

I put back on my glasses, reaching for the microphone. I grip the handle like a lifeline. I'm thankful for my foresight to ask Charlee to serve as the MC. All I have to do is introduce her and pass the mic. It feels impossible when I can't stop replaying my conversation with Max. He's back, but it's only temporary. That's a sign, right?

I fall back. *Count to ten, stand up, and get this started.* And whatever I do …don't look at row twelve on the left-hand side, I reason around the insane throne in my head.

21

"Ten minutes." Chase echoes over my shoulder. "I can do it for you, Parker."

"I got it."

It's showtime. I stand between the front seats bringing the microphone to my mouth.

"Welcome to the Freedom Tour with Parker Belle Realty." I smile, waiting for the applause to die out. "You will see beautiful homes, sip the best wines, eat the bests foods. Today, you are my very special guests."

I scan the rows making eye contact with each guest, a decision I immediately regret when I stop at row twelve seat one, Max, then seat two Stephanie. I hold his eyes for a moment too long as a sensuous energy passes between us. I have to lean into the seat for support.

"Thankfully you're not stuck with me all day." I speak around the fist, lodged in my throat. "I'd like for my guys to stand." I swing an open hand in front of me as the guys stand. "These are our beautiful tour guides. No question is too small." They wave and sit. "But our party wouldn't be complete without our beautiful, colorful, and absolutely vibrant host, Charlee Grant."

The applause fills the bus, and she walks in my direction. The bus slows to a stop.

"I will turn you over to her very capable hands. Thank you."

I drop in the seat. The heat in Max's eyes felt like a spotlight shining in my direction. The animated quality in Charlee's voice fades into the background. I grab my iPad to distract myself. Facts, figures, square footage but it can't drown out desire, lust, love.

How can I still love him? He left when all I wanted was a few years to get myself established. It's best I remember it's always his way or no way. I've come too far, worked too hard.

The doors open and Charlee leads our guests out of the bus. The brush of people moving pulls me from the haze of Maximus Bradley until I feel him lower into the seat beside me.

I wouldn't consider myself a praying woman, not by a long shot, but I prayed. Prayed God wouldn't let this man rip my broken heart out of my chest again. I have to take control of this situation now.

"Look, Max, I overreacted. You're my guest, and I apologize for being..." I search for the word, making sure I don't gaze into his dark eyes.

"Unreasonable?"

"No..."

"Excessive?"

"No...you came up here. I didn't go back there." I turn towards him, remembering I can't look this man in the eyes. I stare straight ahead.

The bus is silent.

"Jealous?"

Without thinking, my eyes find his. The unrelenting shine causes lust to flow through my body. I open and close my mouth to refute his assessment. But the word ramps up the rate of my heartbeat, he's right.

I'm jealous. Damn it. Why did he have to come back, today of all days?

"Maybe it's the beard." He offers.

I laugh, and I can't help it. He's a magnet. I check out his beard, covering the lower part of his square jaw. He is beautiful. His olive, sun-kissed skin. His dark, dreamy eyes. His firm lips.

I exhale. "Maybe. Look, I gotta go."

I stand, and he wraps a hand around my forearm. My entire body tingles at his touch, and I hate its betrayal. He pulls me back to the seat, and immediately, his mouth covers mine. His mouth is tender and familiar yet different. I lean in greedily wanting more than I should, wanting what I shouldn't.

We pull apart.

Breathing in unison. Eyes locked. Then the though assaults me, *and I love Max*. A soft gasp escapes, and he reads me like a book.

"Parker?"

"I'll be there Chase." I break his hold, and I take the moment to escape.

"This isn't over Parker."

"Actually it is."

His head jerks back.

"Don't act surprised. Was I jealous? Yes, I've never like Stephanie and the man I thought I'd love forever pops up after eight years…with her. Hell, yeah, I felt some kind of way. But we both know it won't go anywhere."

"Are you sure about that?" His finger traces down the

side of my face, and I can't move. "I recall you once saying you'd always love me."

"And I still do."

My words surprise us both. I jump to my feet using his shock as a means of escape. Anguish is buried in my chest where hope once lived. I feel hands grip my shoulders. I spin around, ready to face off with Max and see my guys.

"I can't do this. Why did he have to come back today? Now?" I glance around disoriented.

"Baby I'm sorry to be the one to tell you, but this is not the time to freak the fuck out." Charlee steps forward. The sea of guys parts and she pulls me to her chest. "I can bull shit with the best of them. But if you expect me to sell this million-dollar house, you might as well take my bank card."

I laugh through my tears.

"The guests are walking through the house. We have only a few minutes before you're up. What can we do?"

"I got this. Just give me a second." Charlee passes me the microphone heading into the house.

"You have ten minutes. I'll get the guys set up." Chase assures me, leaving me alone.

I don't bounce around aimless in my life. I'm about goals, targets, deadlines. I pull out my phone, revisiting my goals for the day.

I want to submit at least one offer.

I want ten solid contacts.

I want to scout prospects for Platinum Prestige.

I'm feeling better already. I head back to the bus to get the specs for the house. Minutes later, I'm inside.

"Our first home was built in 2003 and sits on ten acres of land coming in just under eight thousand square feet. This rustic beauty has five bedrooms, seven bathrooms, and a four-car garage. If you want to see my favorite feature, meet me in the family room."

I hit my stride. My signature tour starts with the view. I am a significant competitor in this market, not because I sell the most homes, but because I sell high-end properties. Most of my clients sign exclusive contracts with me because I deliver.

There are thousands of homes on the market. But very few compare to the view of the Austin Hill Country. And nobody knows Austin like me.

I know the benefits of raising a family here. I know the value of buying property in this market, at this time. I know it because I was born and raised here. Hell, I'll probably die here.

I love this city, and it shows in the number of families I place in their dream homes.

I wait in the living room, and I lose myself in the moment. The specs and details roll off my tongue, and I'm in my zone. Hunter and Jordan stand on either side of the patio doors. I nod and the doors open.

A gasp rings through the room. The bright blue sky and rolling green hills bring a smile to my face. I stroll around the pool that drops off into the horizon. I point out the features, answer questions, and then I stand back.

"Ladies and gentlemen, this is just the beginning. Shall we?"

We walk every square inch of the house. It takes thirty minutes, and I leave them alone to explore. I visit my favorite nooks and crannies of the house while I wait.

I feel better, more in control of my response to Max.

"You're a brilliant woman."

I spin around and smile at the man heading in my direction. "I'm a fan of compliments, but what brought this on?"

Liam steps forward, "I'm assuming you intentionally sold the tickets in pairs."

"You would be correct. It limits the decision time if both husband and wife are present."

"And you started with the most expensive house first?"

"Very astute, Mr. Walsh. The others are great. But none of them compare to this."

He laughs. "I have one final question."

"And that is?"

"Is that a helicopter pad over there?"

I glance over my shoulder and nod. "Once again, you're correct. Should I start on the paperwork?"

"Yes ma'am, and don't tell my wife. She about passed out when I bought another jet."

I laugh, "I'll see what I can do."

He strolls off searching for Harper and I yelp. This is a six-million-dollar house. I dance in place, not caring that my feet are screaming for mercy from these heels.

"You really do know your stuff."

I spin around, and time stops. "You doubted?"

Max chuckles, looking over me seductively, and I squeeze my thighs together. Fire races through my body, and I can't stop the flow of my thoughts.

He crosses the threshold closing the door behind him. I give his body a bold sweeping gaze from his curly hair to the tips of his polished shoes. Each passing second steals my breath.

Broad shoulders. Powerful build. Intentional steps.

Max strolls in slow motion until my back is against the wall pinned beneath his heavy body. I shouldn't want him. But I do. Running seems futile.

"We have a problem." His eyes darken with desire but lurking in the depths I recognize an ache similar to my own. "I love you, Parker. But loving you isn't good for me."

CHAPTER 4

I whispered the words, but I can't stop kissing her. I blame the gloss on her soft lips or her soft moans of pleasure. I yearn to hear it more. So, I find ways to slip off from Stephanie to corner Parker in every house.

The guest bedroom. The pantry. The garage.

We're now in an amazing master bathroom with marble countertops and black tile. But it's the glass paired with large mirrors that make me surrender. Against my will, this bathroom makes me envision Parker showering and me seeing every inch of her naked body until I join her.

This is our home.

I blink out of my stupor as the crowd disperses. I wait until I have her alone, closing the door behind us. I turn the lock, unable to think logically. What if we have this moment to revisit...*us?*

Parker turns slowly, her eyes bouncing from me to the locked door. I removed my jacket, letting it fall to the floor. I take steps closing the distance between us.

Her hands reach for the opening of her blazer, shrugging out of it. I appreciate the fit of the t-shirt across her full breasts. I easily place her to the counter between the his and her sinks as my pulse quickens with longing for her. I can't wait. I need to taste her now.

I grip her hips and pull her to my throbbing cock. Her back arches and the soft groan makes me smile.

"Parker open your eyes and listen to me." Her lazy eyes bounce open. I kiss the end of her nose. "When's the last time you've been with someone?"

Her eyes widen with shock. I lick my lips, letting her know precisely what I have in mind.

"A year." Her airy response is etched in need. "And you?"

"Longer than six months. Maybe seven."

I place a trail of kisses up the side of her neck until my mouth finds hers. Her command of a room, pointing out the hardwood floors, the stainless steel, the imported fixtures. I'll never see house hunting the same. The delicate way her hand ran the length of the kitchen island made me so hard it hurt to walk. She cups my face bringing my eyes to hers.

"Why?"

"I'm tired of settling."

Her legs wrap around my waist, crushing her body

into mine. We grind like teenagers, and I ache to be inside her. Our kisses go from tame to flaming hot in seconds. Her wild, hot hands tug at my shirt.

"Baby, you can't rip my shirt off."

"Why?" She groans.

I laugh, locking her delicate wrists with one hand behind her back. "Because you have to work, and I can't walk around with a jacket and no shirt. But first, I want a sample."

I lift the hem of her shirt thankful for the perfection of her brown skin and the chocolate morsels I take into my mouth.

"Max…"

Parker thrusts her breasts closer to my willing mouth, and I feast like a man starving. I go from one to the next, but I want more.

"How much time do we have?" I stretch out between kisses.

"Ten tops." She bites into the tender flesh at the base of my neck.

Animal hunger takes over. "Stand up. Are you as sweet as I remember?"

I STAND ON WOBBLY LEGS. I blink, and my pants are around my ankles, and my bare ass is on the cold counter. My thighs are wrapped around his neck.

"Parker." The heat from his breath makes me want to

close my legs until he swipes a long lick. I buck in response as his tongue plays with my clit. Then his thumb dips inside me.

"Max…"

His fingers dig into my heat, the more he explores, the wider I open for him. He frees my hands to run through his thick hair. Max was my first lover. The one who showed me the highs and lows of love. But our lovemaking compares to none.

Today, he teased and teased until I couldn't resist. Stolen kisses and gentle brushes of his hand had me ready to toss my doubts aside.

"Baby, we have to go." He insists kissing my left and right thigh, then darting his tongue deep one more time.

"I'm so close. Not yet."

He laughs, and I want to scream. I feel the end calling me closer, and I don't care if my clients are on the other side of the door. I've waited years for this for him.

"Babe, one time and we'll have to finish this later." He lowers me to the floor, turning me to face the mirror behind the sinks.

"Tonight?" My eyes meet his and hope stirs inside of me. "Are you sure?"

"I never had doubts about us. This is your call." He uses his foot to spread my feet wider apart.

We had a love that was deep and wide and all-consuming. Can we find it again? I'm not sure, but Max knows his way around my body, and I'll let later take care of later.

"Yes, Max and for the record, I didn't doubt us. I merely asked for more time."

He stands behind me, our eyes locked in the reflection. His hand braces against the mirror and the other slips in front of my body, between my thighs, and his fingers enter me. I buck, throwing my ass back, his eyes never leaving mine.

"Parker, promise me." His kisses whisper across my skin taking command over my body.

"What Max?" Stars cloud my vision. My head falls back to his shoulder, unable to resist the pleasure he's giving.

"That we'll do whatever it takes to make us work." My head pops up, eyes wide. "Promise."

The tempo increases, I'm teetering on the edge of sane and insane, sober and intoxicated, and I want it all.

My man. My career. My business. My happily ever after.

"I promise."

"Thank you, tesoro mio."

His treasure. I thought I'd never hear the words directed at me or that it would mean the world to me. The mounting pressure explodes, and I struggle to maintain my clarity. My screams are muffled in his mouth, and I feel relieved and selfish.

...loving you isn't good for me.

His declaration rings in my head, and I mentally add one more goal to my list. I have to show Max that loving him is what I was made to do. That together, we can have it all.

"Parker, I want this house."

esoro mio. Max's Italian roots was always a turn on. I heard him say it for years until his mother translated it for me.

His treasure. It's the sweetest sentiment, but it rubs against the source of all of my romantic woes. I never want to be someone's treasure at the expense of letting go of my individuality.

My own finances. My own career. My own life. But I want Max. I can't let my only child tendencies to ruin a chance at correcting our past.

I run downstairs to rejoin the tour. Max removed his undershirt and cleaned my body. Then I left him alone upstairs to tour the house alone. The bottom is in sight, and my guys erect a barrier, blocking my escape.

"How was the master bathroom?" Chase asks, and she can barely hide the smirk.

"Max decided to place an offer on this house."

"I bet…he…did." Charlee shakes her rump from side to side.

I glaze over my shoulder, ensuring Max isn't around. "We're going to try to work it out."

Harper does an uncoordinated shimmy and laughs.

"What about his sidekick?" Ryann steps forward.

We glance toward the living room at Stephanie. She's eyeing me big time.

"We could leave her…accidentally, of course." Jordan chuckles.

"No ma'am. No man or woman left behind. What does she do?" Harper turns to the group dropping her voice.

"I think she's a lawyer or lobbyist," Ryann says.

"I'm over it. I don't even know what started it. Either way, let's get through this day without drama."

"What about test driving the bathrooms?"

"Charlee." We say in unison.

"Y'all act like I'm the only one that's a lady in the streets and a freak in the sheets." She drops to the floor.

"Ahhh, *shyte* baby!" Darius rounds the corner.

I laugh until I cry. "Let's break this freaky party up. We have three more houses left then…."

"S&J here we come."

I MAKE my way back to the bus. The guests are enjoying

cocktails and hors d 'oeuvres before we move on to the next location. I need to transmit the details for Max's offer to the office. I have three full-time staff members that work for me. I'm lucky my guys don't mind working events like this. I knock on the door, and Denzel opens it.

"Parker."

I recognize the voice. I take a deep breath and turn around.

"Stephanie, are you enjoying the tour?" I force a smile on my face. *When they go low, we go high.*

"Why don't you leave Max alone? We had a shot until you decide to give out sexual favors."

"We are two grown-ass women. I don't have time for your rumors or your drama." I step closer. "You know the history between Max and I and you took that chance bringing him on my tour."

"You don't deserve him, Parker. He asked to marry you, and you declined. Let him move on." She walks off, and I see Max standing on the steps of the house.

Stephanie has a point, and I owe Max an explanation. It all seems cut and dry, but it's not. People think because I said no that I didn't love him or that I didn't want to have a relationship with him. But neither are true.

I walk the rest of the distance, stopping at the front porch. I play with the buttons on his shirt.

"Do you have a moment?"

"Step into my office." He gestures to the furniture in the courtyard.

This house is smaller, more intimate. The designs pairs wood floors with creme accents. The owners staged the house with white and gray furniture using the limestone wood-burning fireplaces throughout the house add specks of color.

We sit on the couch overlooking the view. He pulls me close into his side.

"This is an amazing pick." I snuggle closer.

"Can you imagine us spending our evenings out here?"

I think about it, glancing around. The foliage around the house and open floor plan give an openness to the space.

"I can. Wait until you see my place."

"Is it in town?"

"Yes, it's more urban. But equally beautiful." I look out over the treetops. "I owe you an explanation."

"I'd rather not go there."

"But we must." I sit up and turn to face him. "I apologize. You dropped to your knee, and I freaked out. Then you wouldn't let me explain."

"It's hard to explain. 'I can't marry you.'" His face hardens. I cup his face bringing it to me.

"I said, 'I can't marry you yet.' There's a difference." He blinks several times. "I'm sure you'll comb your memory, replaying that day over and over again. We can discuss the details later. Right now, I want you to know I'm sorry for the hurt it caused you and the time we've lost."

I kiss him deeply, from a place of sincerely wanting to move forward, together. I wipe the gloss from his lips.

"I accept under one condition."

"A condition?" I sit back, not liking the intense look on his face.

"Can you do that drop it like it's hot move?" The teasing laughter lingers in his eyes, and I playfully slap his chest.

"I refuse to ruin my knees." I push to my feet, pulling him up. He brushes his thick manhood against my ass, and I make it wiggle to make him laugh again.

We head to the bus. The guys load later with all the equipment loaded in the bottom, and Denzel drives us to the next destination.

Max sits next to me, and we talk, catching up on each other's lives.

I lean into his body, loving his scent. "Tell me about your business."

"I own Wine & Dine Delivery, a food, and beverage delivery company."

"Like a food truck."

"No, think UberEats, GrubHub, and several others. But we specialize in family-owned establishments instead of major chains. We're in several states, and I have my eyes on Texas next. However, it's proving more difficult than I expected."

"Which prompted your move back?"

"Exactly." He kisses my forehead.

"That's interesting. I think I can help." I sit up. "Hunt."

"What's up?" Hunter calls from the back.

"Come up here for a second."

"Wait…where are you going?"

"We had some similar issues with a few of our delivery services in Texas and Louisiana."

"You have food delivery services for a real estate company?"

"No babe, keep up." I chuckle. "I'm an equal partner in Platinum Prestige. It's a concierge service. We service clients across the US, and we're expanding some services overseas."

"And you got clearance in Texas?"

"You're asking the wrong guy." I kiss him and give Hunter my seat. I give him a finger wave and move to the seat with Chase.

The bus moves slowly through traffic. We visit the final houses and unload in front of S&J. I stand outside the bus shaking hands and hugging each guest. I have offers for seven of the ten houses, not a bad day at all.

Stephanie stops in front of me. I extend my hand, and she takes it.

"I'll be in touch," she says, walking away.

I watch her walk away, still baffled how we've always seemed to be on the outs with each other.

"Turns out she's a consultant with a specialty in business expansion." Ryann stands next to me.

"Are you familiar with her firm?"

"Vaguely. I'll call around about her and see if we can't

help Max get clearance to operate in the state. Watch that one."

"Yes, ma'am." Max steps outside and I still can't believe he's here. I move in his direction turning back to Ryann. "Are you joining us?

"No, I'm heading home. I'm up for partner and duty calls."

"I think we need to sign you up for speed dating again."

"Oh, nooo, you don't. Harper found enough losers for all of us. I'm glad you're boo'ed up, but I have no time in my life for a man, at least not regularly. Except when it's time to drop it like it's hot."

I howl. "I'd pay to see you drop it in a suit."

"I'll keep that in mind." She chuckles. "Don't forget, we have a meeting at the new property on Monday."

"I'm there." I pull her into a hug. "Thank you. Love you."

"Love you too. I'm out to find a strong cup of coffee and review some contracts."

"Don't work too hard."

"I'm a black woman gunning for partner in a majority white firm. Hard work is my middle name."

"Ryann 'Hard Work' Gibson, time waits for no woman."

"Go get your man. I bet you a bill they'll name me as the youngest partner in the firm. Time waits for no woman, but I plan to make it my bitch."

We laugh, hugging one more time.

"You've built a full life." Max wraps an arm around me.

"I have." I watch Ryann until she honks her horn driving off into the night. "Are we heading inside or my place? I'm officially done for the day."

"Your place."

CHAPTER 6

"Welcome to my home." I toss my keys on the table. "Would you like a tour?" I reach for my jacket, but Max stops me. His hand glides inside until it topples to the floor.

I lead him inside, stopping when he pulls my shirt off. I stop his hands when they reach for my waistband. I turn around glancing over my shoulder. I unbutton my pants, lowering them to the floor with my ass in his face.

"Fuck…" I hear his growl over the thumping of my heart.

I stand before him in my bra and thong. I loosen the bun on top of my head, letting my curls cascade down my back.

"Alexa play Max's Medley."

A sexy brow arches in disbelief as the room fills with music. I lead him to my couch, pushing him back.

I never forgot him. Tonight, I won't have to pleasure myself with him on my mind. I'll have the real deal in my bed.

The tiredness from today erases the moment I straddle his body, rubbing my moist heat across his thick erection. I rock my body to the music, teasing his mouth with kisses, loving the sting of his smack against my bare ass.

I stand rolling in his face, and he bites my cheek. The sound of his zipper opening rings between the songs. He lifts his hips pushing his pants down. I turn and my mouth waters with anticipation.

"If you keep looking at my shit like that I might explode."

He holds the condom between us. I open it. I roll it slowly down his shaft, it hits the base, and I swirl the tip of his head with my tongue to hear him growl. Then I anchor my hands on his shoulders, guiding him home. The first thrust fills me, and I buckle against him.

"Shit...damn baby." He pulls out and drives deeper. Hitting against my spot and I'm not ready.

"That pussy missed me. Huh..."

"Yes..." I ride until my legs are weak.

"I got you baby."

He flips us, taking my leg over his shoulder. I scream his name like it's my native tongue. His grips on my hips, slapping against my body.

Our pants of pleasure compete with the music. His head falls forward, I reach up, taking his tongue in my mouth. How did I survive for eight years without this? Without him?

The sensation building causes my toes to curl, my spine to bend, and I beg for more. He gives, blowing hot breath in my ear still talking shit and panting my name.

I'm holding on to the edge of my restraint, the end is near. I clench my eyes tight stiffening under him.

"Stop amore mio. Relax." Max chuckles. His strokes are long and deep, rocking our bodies in unison.

"I don't want it to be over yet." I whine.

"Let me hit it the way you like it, baby?"

I open my eyes, and there's a hint of fire staring at me. "Please…"

"Point to the room."

I'm scooped into his arms until he lowers me to the bed, entering me from the back. His muscular body wraps around mine, biting my neck, and I lose it. All the pent-up energy from the day leaves on my body, and I'm nothing but a woman tangled in the bed with the man I love.

His groans fill my ear, and I arch my back, ensuring his cock is deep inside me.

"Parker…"

We surrender together, and I'll never be the same.

"I love you, Parker."

"I love you too." I glance up, realizing I can't mess this up again. I wiggle against him. "Now go to sleep because I need another helping of that."

"Just say the word."

Minutes later, we fall into a deep, peaceful sleep.

PARKER SLEEPS BESIDE ME. Yesterday seems like a dream. I try to piece it together. I guess it was inevitable. All her favorites hit me the moment I entered her, and I realized I've always held back a part of myself. A part of me that belongs to Parker.

I fell stupid hard for her before. She had my mind and heart locked to the point of losing myself in my grief. I gave her everything, and she chose her career over us. I can't forget it. But we can always build something new, together.

"Ready to talk?"

"Parker, I don't want to know if it will make me change my mind about us." I glance over and back to the ceiling.

She sits up, crossing her legs, and I wrap the blanket around her.

"I realized after you left that I put independent and dependence on the same level."

"What?" I sit up, my back to her.

"That saying 'I do' would be the first step to losing the parts of me that make me, me."

"What does that mean? Loving me would be the death of you?"

"Basically."

I listen bewildered. The view of the pool from this room is fantastic. I can see the stars dancing off the water. I have two choices to stay and listen or leave and not come back. A second chance is all I have because having her again to lose her seems like a sick joke.

Dig to the source, a small voice whispers. Much like bringing my business to Texas. I can't take no as no. No is usually predicated on something else.

"Do you only feel that way about marriage?"

"I...I guess."

"How many married people do you know?"

"My parents and several of the guys are married now."

"Did they die when they got married? I don't know all of your guys well, but Charlee seems like the Charlee I met in high school. Granted she has a little more sass." I laugh.

"I guess...marriage made them better. Like Harper. She's just as loving and kind. But marrying Liam made her bold and a fighter."

Now we're getting somewhere. I fall back against the bed, pulling her with me.

"What about Hunter?"

"Hunter bloomed. I think motherhood made her less selfish, more giving, and she's absolutely fearless. She has the twins and Zoe." She smiles up at me, and I see the happiness on her face.

"What about...who do you have left?"

"Uh...Taylor is the epitome of love. She and Zach

weathered a hard year, last year. But now, they're a tower of strength and wholeness."

"That doesn't sound like death to me tesoro mio. It sounds like a new beginning."

"It does, doesn't it."

I nod. "My example of marriage is my parents. They're not perfect, but I couldn't imagine one without the other. And I always aspired to have that sort of relationship in my life. What about your parents? How are they?"

"They're the same. But…"

"But what?"

She flips onto her back with her head against my chest. "I believe my mother lost a piece of herself in marriage. She followed my father's dreams and passions instead of her own."

We've hit pay dirt.

"What do you see for yourself, Parker? What are your dreams and passions?"

Parker takes a deep breath. I focus on knowing every word at this moment is crucial because it will determine whether I can have Parker for a season or a lifetime.

"I guess I want what my friends have. Not their relationships but the essence of it." She plays with the ends of her hair.

"And what's that Parker, specifically?"

"I want my career and a partner who loves me, protects me and gives me enough room to spread my wings."

Relief passes through my body. I place a finger beneath her chin, turning her face to me.

"Let me be that for you amore mio."

CHAPTER 7

et me be that for you. I sent an SOS text the moment Max jumps in the shower. S&J isn't opened yet, and my house is usually the alternate meeting place.

I send Ryann a direct text, *Can we meet at your place?*

Certainly, send the brunch roll call, she responds.

Brunch at Ryann's @ 9. Whatcha bringing? I hit send and hurry to respond. *Paper stuff.*

I laugh. None of us are great cooks.

You're going to hell. Cheating on a Sunday. I'll bring the joe. Charlee replies.

The others fall in line. Bagels, donuts, juice, fruit, and within minutes we have a spread. I throw on my sweats and wait in the living room for Max.

He comes out in a Platinum Prestige t-shirt and his dress pants. I giggle.

"Do guys have a walk of shame?"

"The walk of what?" He shakes his head, kissing me before dropping to the couch beside me.

"Walk of shame. It's when you get caught in the clothes you had on last night."

"Nah, guys see it as a badge of honor. I put in work to rock your t-shirt this morning. Say I'm lying."

"I'm done with this conversation."

"I didn't put in work?"

"Max, what do you have planned today?"

"I'm heading to my folks, and I have a day of meetings tomorrow. I recall someone screaming, and I know it wasn't me."

"Now I know it's time to go."

He laughs, and I throw a pillow at him. "I have no problem with admitting you had me saying your name."

Then the fool starts singing Destiny Child. "It's time for you to go."

"I'll leave if you kiss me goodbye." I lean forward and kiss him. His face is somber. "Are we good?"

"We are excellent. Want to connect tomorrow?"

"Absolutely."

THIRTY MINUTES later I'm at Ryann's with the guys. The food is spread out across the coffee table, and we're scattered around the room, waiting for me.

I'm low-key freaking out again. Harper reaches for my hand, and I accept her comfort.

"Eight years ago, Max asked me to marry him, and I

told him not yet. He took it as no, and we went our separate ways."

I stand up and pace the floor.

"I thought I said no because I wanted to build my career on my own before getting married. But after talking with Max this morning, I realize it's more. In my head, I saw marriage as the death of me." I air-quote death.

"Why would you think that?" Harper asks.

"My mother."

The exchange glances. I'm thankful I don't see judgment.

"Your mother is happy. Right?" Payton asks.

"She is, but she's basically a female version of my father."

Ryann leans forward. "You see this as a negative characteristic of marriage?"

"Yes, I don't want to lose my life, my friends, my business because I get married."

"And now?" Hunter asks.

"I have to figure out how to balance the life I lived with my parents against the picture of marriage you all present."

"Then you're cured." Charlee deducts.

"It's not that easy. All men are not like your husbands." I glance around the room.

"Yeah, but Max seems like a cool guy." Chase adds.

"What if I get married and I turn into a mini Max?"

"That's easy. We'd have to get you a good weave and

some padding." They laugh, and I want to throttle Charlee. "I'm joking. You are sitting here talking about marrying the man. Have you even gone on a date yet?"

"No." Maybe I'm overreacting again.

"What about if we promise to tell you if we see you changing for the worst?" Harper suggests.

"But isn't change inevitable in any relationship?" Alex pulls her legs beneath her on the couch. "We all change a little to make room in our lives for new experiences."

I sit back nibbling on a bagel.

Ryann turns in my direction. "I think the real topic here is whether you're willing to try Parker."

THE TOPIC of our brunch transitions from my love life to our quest to find an adequate building to purchase.

I listen as the guys list our requirements. I search the available listings on my computer.

"What if the current place fell through to keep us mobile?" Hunter asks.

"I think it's an accurate assessment. Buying a building will limit us. We're working to operate virtually. A building will tie us Austin."

"I don't see that as a bad thing." Harper says.

"That's because Liam's business is here too. I loved being mobile while working from San Francisco." Charlee adds.

Taylor nods. "Me too."

"What are we saying?" I sit back.

"I think we need a general meeting space. The caliber of our clients is increasing." Hunter states.

"But we can meet at their offices. Which will make us appear more accommodating without the additional overhead." Ryann offers, and the guys nod.

"Let's run a test. Ninety days of continuing without an office. I'll find a shared space as a backup, and if push comes to shove, we have my conference room and the VIP room at S&J."

We agree and shortly after the meeting is closed out and I head to my parents' house. I've discussed the Max situation with my guys. I'm curious about how my parents will react.

CHAPTER 8

The shift in Austin takes me by surprise. The highway extensions, the construction, the business opportunities. Growing up, it was all tech and politics, but now it's a melting pot of cultures and commerce. The pace feels much slower than I expected, which makes it a perfect place for my parents, as for me, after a month here, I find myself missing the hustle of NYC.

I arrive at Parker Belle Realty to snag Parker for lunch. She also has a few more home options for me to review. The other house deal fell through, but my lady is scouting other options. But it seems like buying a spot here will have to wait.

I've been in and out of strategy sessions, and it turns out that talking with Hunter and Ryann on the tour was helpful. I spent the past few weeks in conference calls and meetings with Stephanie developing an approach for the next legislative session. But want I want most is to nail down Parker and it seems scheduling this house tour is the only way to make that happen.

The environment shifts from all city to all Parker. The office is open with glass where walls should be. The spots of greenery make the space feel natural and welcoming. Her receptionist nods as I approach but doesn't bother to get up. This is the only way to spend time with Parker during the daylight hours. She works nonstop between showing houses and Platinum Prestige.

I use a knuckle to knock on her door. She waves me inside, talking into the phone. I remove my jacket tossing it in the seat beside me. She holds up a finger signaling she'll need a minute I respond to text messages and emails until I realize it's been forty-five minutes. She mouths, "Sorry, can I call you?"

She returns to her conversation, not waiting for my reply. And this is a mirror of our "dating" for the past month. I need to find food. I step outside as my phone rings, and I don't recognize the local number.

"Are you available for lunch?" It's Darius Grant, Charlee's husband, and the man is right on time.

"I am. What do you have in mind?"

We talk, and he gives me the address to S&J. I enter the place minutes later. I see a few familiar faces standing with Darius. He quickly runs through the introductions.

"This place smells amazing."

He chuckles, turning me down a walkway. "Wait until you step outside."

The doors to the courtyard open, and I feel like I'm back in NYC. I scan the open area with a handful of food trucks.

Darius stands back. "What do you have a taste for? I eat more barbecue than I should, but everything here is delicious."

"How about Thai?"

"Thai it is."

We grab our food and head back inside. The food is better than expected, and I relax appreciating the music.

"How's it going?" Darius asks the moment I push my plate away. The man has an easy-going nature that makes me feel as if I've known him forever.

"Business is good. Adjusting to life back in Austin, not as good as I'd like."

"This isn't New York at all. But it might help to do more than sit in meetings all day."

"Yeah, it seems the timing of the legislative session had us scrambling to meet with a few elected officials. Plus trying to keep up with Parker."

"Miss Parker …how's that going?"

I shrug not sure how much I want to reveal. "It's going. How does Charlee balance her work with Delicious Chocolates and Platinum Prestige?"

He leans back. "It depends. They seem to have a lot of their operation automated, and once we had DJ, she works primarily from the house. They have meetings when going after large accounts and she travels from time to time. But we manage. Are you feeling the difference between your relationship before and your relationship now?"

Darius and I didn't hang out in high school, but I recall he and Charlee dating when Parker and I dated. Then I went off to college, and after Parker and I didn't work out, I moved to New York.

"Yes, more than I anticipated."

"Want to talk about it?"

"Between us?" I lean forward.

"No doubt."

"I love her, and she loves me. But…"

Darius is a man of few words. He laughs freely, and his love for his wife and family are crystal clear. "You wonder if you fit."

"Exactly." I exhale. I struggle for the past week, trying to pinpoint what it is.

"It's to be expected. Parker has a full life. She's running a million-dollar real estate company and an active partner in another. Have you talked to her about it?"

"I've tried."

"Try harder. Our relationships are similar. We dated as teens and young adults. But coming back together as adults, you'll learn our women are fiercely independent and not because they have to, but because they want to."

"Yeah, but is that what I want?"

"Only you can decide and be honest. I hate the years I spent apart from Charlee. The distance in space and time meant we had to decide how we wanted to build a life together."

"Do you regret moving your business to Austin?"

"Not at all. We spent several years commuting between here and San Francisco. My parents are here, her parents are here, her business is here, plus her guys are here." He looks me dead in my eyes. "And listen, they are a package deal. Charlee and Taylor moved to California for a while but flew back often."

"And how is that?"

He shrugs. "It's Charlee. I appreciate the guys having my lady's back. So, know, when you enter a relationship with her, it's more than the teenage love we once knew."

I stare at the grooves in the table. His words hit home as the tension between Parker and me grows. Her life is filled with family, friends, and her business. It makes me wonder whether she has room for me too.

"Is it worth it?" I ask.

"Yes…a million times over."

The conversation moves on until we stand to leave. He gives me a brotherly hug, and we plan to hang out again with the rest of the fellas, as he calls them.

I leave S&J with more questions than answers. I love Parker, but can I trust that our past won't repeat itself.

I pull out my phone to call her.

"Hey, you." I hear the smile in her voice.

"Hey, I'm outside S&J and thought I'd swing back by your office."

"I have a closing tonight. But if you can hang tight, I'll head over when I'm done."

"Then we can head to my place?" I offer wanting her all to myself.

"I cleared my weekend. I'll be all yours."

"That's what I like to hear. Handle your business, and I'll be here waiting."

"WOULD YOU LIKE A REFILL?"

I glance up at the bartender, shaking my head. It's after eight, and my text messages and calls to Parker remain unanswered. I stand laying cash on the bar for my tab and his tip.

"Calling it a night so early?"

I glance over my shoulder and see Stephanie. "I am. How about you?"

"I'm here for the live music. Care to join me?"

I check the time, and it's been hours. I consider Parker for a moment. Last time she saw Stephanie, it wasn't pleasant. She's been cool with me consulting with her for business, but I'd hate for her to get the wrong impression.

"Thanks for the offer but I have plans."

"Suit yourself." She heads off towards the courtyard.

I send another text to Parker, *I'm heading out.*

I'll be there in fifteen, she responds.

I find an empty table in the lounge. Live music and a night out with my lady seems like the perfect way to end the week. The band starts their first set, and I sit back appreciating the vibe of this place.

"Got a few minutes?"

"A few, Parker is headed over."

Stephanie sits across from me with her food, and we discuss the progress of the project.

"I doubt we get much done until the session starts in January."

"What do you suggest?" I struggle to hide my frustration.

"I suggest loading our gun with the right ammo and people. I can get on the calendars of as many representatives and congressmen as possible. Then we can gauge their interest and create a plan to support the other initiatives that favor getting Wine & Dine Delivery here."

"I hate the thought of putting it off for another six months." I sit back.

"Consistency is crucial with any expansion, especially one that may require lobbying for legislative change."

We seem to make progress then it's slammed to a screeching halt. But Stephanie has proved herself in the short while we've worked together. She's the official liaison for this rollout, and I have to trust her judgment, it's why I pay her.

"What's the estimated timeline?"

"Under perfect conditions, this time next year. Will you hang around in this area?"

"Am I needed here?"

"Not really with video conferencing and my team locally. I'd guess you'll need to return here and there. But I don't expect much activity until February or March."

"I'll weigh my options and keep you posted."

We talk, and I notice once again Parker is a no show. The band takes the stage and let the soul music mask my disappointment. I glance at my phone, hoping to see a text message. She hasn't reached out, and I'm not about to either. She'll call when she's ready.

I glance across the table at Stephanie. "What made you decide to shift from practicing law to starting a consulting firm?"

CHAPTER 9

I stare at my phone, blinking to bring the picture into focus. The benefit and disadvantage living life in a tight circle of friends and family is your business is never truly your business.

A stare at Max and Stephanie having dinner, and I have to decide on my next move. I expand the picture brushing my fingers across the screen of my phone. Yes, that's him and *her*. I swipe through the others. Them leaning close together. Him laughing. Her smiling up at him, and I recognize the look in her eyes.

I rub my eyes glancing at the time before dialing his number, not sure what I'll say.

"Hello." The sound of sleep lingers in his voice, and for a moment, I wish I was there instead of here, still working.

"Busy?"

"Nah, what time is it?" I hear him move around.

"Ten after midnight… Are you alone?" I place the call on speaker to look at the pictures again.

"What?" His voice cuts through the silence in my office.

"You heard me, are you alone?"

"Are you fucking serious right now, Parker?" His laughter is gruff and lacks any resemblance of humor.

"As a heart attack." I stand picking up my phone from the desk. "I'm on my way."

"Don't do me any favors." His voice is cold and exact. "You call five hours late trying to check my whereabouts."

"It didn't take long for you to find a willing substitute."

"What are you talking about? Please clue me in on the shit going on in your head."

"You and Stephanie." A cold knot forms in my stomach. I grab my purse and keys heading for the door.

"What do you have, spies, watching me?"

"No, I have friends concerned about seeing my man cozied up with *her*."

"I call you nonstop all day, and you don't stop to respond to a single message, but you hear about me having a conversation with Stephanie, and you finally pick up the phone."

My heart drops stunned by his words. "I got—"

"Tied up. The problem is you're always tied up. Showing houses, Platinum Prestige, babysitting, guy SOS calls."

"I will not choose between my life and you." I'm yelling to match pace with him.

"If that's all you got out of this conversation, I'll talk with you later. Good night Parker."

"Max…"

I stop on the sidewalk outside my office. I lock the doors and minutes later I ring the doorbell to his suite. The evidence stacked against me doesn't look good. But this is my life, and he didn't explain why he was having dinner with Stephanie if he was supposedly waiting around for me.

Max opens the door, and I want to quiet the storm raging in his eyes. His chest is bare, and his boxers hang low on his hips. He doesn't say a word.

I close the door behind us, dropping my purse and keys on the table. He falls to the couch, his hair is wild, and I stop waiting, for what I don't know.

I don't believe he has an interest in Stephanie, but it doesn't lessen the sting of seeing the pictures. I want him inside me. It could be the green-eyed monster or a slight acknowledgment that he's trying, and I still feel the need to run.

I'm going to lose him again.

I can't let that happen. I remove my blouse, and I toss my bra at him. Then I reach for my pants, closing the distance between us.

"Help me."

"You can't cover every issue with sex Parker."

I stand between his outstretched legs and lower my

zipper. I run my fingers through his hair, bringing him to me. He kisses my stomach, running his hands over my ass and slowly pulling down my pants and my panties. I step out, one leg at a time.

His hot breath brushing against my thighs, my heat, makes me wet. A large palm to my stomach is the only command I receive as I sit on the table. He places a foot on either side of his body, and I'm stretched wide, ready, for him.

His eyes cloud in a sexual haze, lowering to his knees. He teases me while holding me in place with the questions in his eyes. I know I'm failing at repairing this relationship, and I can't seem to help myself.

His fingers part my folds and a bold swipe of his tongue erases everything but the man giving absolute pleasure. I arch into him, crying out. Then he enters me. Our bodies join as one, skin to skin. Hard strokes rock the table, and I lift my hips meeting each thrust matching his hunger.

My core tightens, and through a breathy moan, I tell him I can't take anymore.

"Then come for me amore mio."

I don't expect the soul-shattering release. Maybe it's the fight. Maybe it's having him uninhibited. Maybe it's knowing that I'm quitting again, and I don't want to lose him because I love him. My life feels complete with him here. But I can't rely on a man for my happiness. Not even Max.

. . .

I CARRY Parker to the bathroom and run us a bath. The moment we lower into the hot water, I know I have to leave Austin and me going could be the end of us.

"Parker, I'm going back to New York."

Her body stiffens. "When?"

"Today."

The silence is filled with rage and agony and love. I drop my head back against the cold tile, praying this is the right decision. But I know staying will lead to me one day resenting that I have to compete for a place in her life.

"Why?" Her voice is low and distant.

"Because I don't belong here. Plus, my team can handle the rest of my business affairs."

"But what about us?" She whispers.

"What about us?"

Parker turns in the tub glancing back at me with a shadow of the inner turmoil that's ruining any chance that we have to make this relationship work.

"Come with me."

"I can't."

"Correction, you won't."

Her silence pokes at my uncertainties regarding my place in her life. Her response at this moment will determine the fate of our relationship.

"My business, my family, my friends are here.

"My…my…my…. you sound like a broken record. At what point do you consider us, we, anything or anybody except for yourself?"

"I told you I have a full life. What do you want a got-damn babysitter?"

The echoes of our voices fill the room. *How did we get here?*

I don't want to hurt her, and I don't want to tell her goodbye. But we've crossed a line, and there's no coming back.

"Parker, I never asked for anything, but you. Apparently, that was too much to ask."

"So, when you leave, that's it?" Her eyes hold mine.

"Yes, if you're not coming with me."

She pushes to the opposite end of the tub. "That's not fair, Max."

"Tough."

My heart is erecting a shield to protect me from the fallout of this one. It took years to get over her before, and like an idiot, I believed she was ready this time.

"What you're asking for is impossible?"

"Then say goodbye now and save both of us the fucking heartbreak."

CHAPTER 10

*M*ax left. By the time I climbed out of the bathtub, he was gone. I dressed, and now I'm sitting outside in my parent's driveway. Saturdays in the Hamilton start early. I walk to the door using my key.

"Mom," I call out.

"Come upstairs."

I drop my stuff and run up the stairs, past my old bedroom. I look inside the master suite.

"Good morning." I lean in and kiss her cheek.

"Same to you. Are you all right honey? It's not often you stop by on a Saturday morning."

I shake my head, I'm not all right. I sit on the edge of her bed, watching her add foundation to her face. Our eyes meet in the reflection, and she turns around.

"What is it?" She crosses the room and sits beside me.

"Max is leaving today." I brush away the tears. Why am I crying? I knew this would happen.

"Start at the beginning."

"I don't want to hold you up." I stand.

"Sit down Parker. Stop trying to be tough and let me at least listen." Her hands drop to her lap, and I sit back beside her.

"Things got worse after our last talk. I've been closing the houses from the tour and looking for potential options for Platinum Prestige and …" I reach for a tissue. "He says I didn't have room in my life for him."

"Well, did you?"

"I tried." I shrug.

"What does that mean, honey?"

I scan my mind. He was the one visiting my office, coming by my place, inviting me out. I'd agree to meet him then get caught up with a client or something requiring my attention.

"I told him my life was busy."

"Then it's obviously not the right time."

"How can you say that Mom?"

"Because if it were the right time, you'd *make* time."

"And ignore all of my other responsibilities?" I fold over exhausted with it all. "I can't sit around babysitting a grown man."

"It's not babysitting but showing Max that he's a priority." Her voice drops.

I glance at my hands. "It all sounds like a bunch of coddling to me. Why does love require women to walk away from everything while the man sacrifices nothing?"

"Where'd you learn that absurd logic?"

"From you, Mom."

My mother turns, and I expect to see anger or shock instead, she laughs.

"Please tell me this story."

"Mom, it's not funny."

"Girl, you always manage to concoct a wild story that only you know the beginning, middle, and end to. So, please tell me how I've walked away from everything and how your father has sacrificed nothing."

"Mom, you never had an interest in real estate, and you walked away from your job as a teacher to follow Daddy's dream."

"Correction, I left teaching to raise my child. I got my real estate license to help my husband build a legacy for our family. It just so happened that I was extremely good at it and made good money doing it. Continue."

I consider her words for a moment before moving forward. "Dad got to travel and go to business meetings and hang with his friends while you stayed in the background."

"Correction, your father worked twelve to sixteen-hour days to pay for private school, specialty camps, summer trips with your friends, college. Should I continue?"

"No, ma'am. But it always appeared, to me, that you sat back letting him call the shots."

"Parker, there is nothing wrong with sitting back, letting your man call the shots when you find a man worth following. I never had to worry about my husband in another woman's bed, about whether we'd have money to care for our house or our family."

Images of my parents over the years surface rounding out the picture she's casting.

"My husband had a vision for his life and a vision for our family. And I gladly followed him because when you find that man, the right man, everything about your life will be better. Not because of him, but because as a unit you're stronger, more powerful than you are as individuals."

"I'm sorry Mom."

"Don't be sorry, do better. Marriage is not a chore, but it's not that complicated. I tried to stay out of your relationship business, but since you're in my room, on my time, I'm about to add my two cents. That man adored you. But no amount of love can be showered on a person with their mind set on doing things her own way."

"Mom…" She stands up and sits back at the vanity. "So, what you're saying is…"

"You're selfish. I played my part. You had us all to yourself. You got anything you wanted. And now you have your friends. But when you go home at night, after conquering the world, who do you want waiting on the other side of that door?"

I COULDN'T HANDLE the fire hydrant my mother spewed

in my direction. So, I did what I do best, I work. For the past six months, I fill my calendar up with showings and closings and enough commercial deals to leave me with no time to think about Max or the fact that I hurt the one man I love, again.

But it doesn't work because he still invades my dreams and I wake up crying like today. I drag out of bed, and I turn on the tv to drown out my thoughts.

"A group of third-party food delivery services was successful in their attempts to change the laws in the state of Texas."

I sit on the edge of the couch, waiting to hear Wine & Dine Delivery mentioned, and Max's company is part of those credited by the reporter.

"This means Texas can order dinner and alcoholic beverages from the comfort of their homes. I think I'll order enchiladas and a margarita for dinner tonight." The anchor laughs, signing off.

This is a major win for Max. I stare at my phone, wondering if I should text or call. I hit his number on speed dial.

"Congratulations, Max." I hold the line as emotions overtake me. "Miss you. Love you. Bye."

I turn off the tv, pulling my curtains closed and I crawl back into bed wondering if sleep can heal a broken heart.

CHAPTER 11

"Get up, Parker!"

Light floods my room. I toss the blanket over my head. "Charlee go home, and Taylor leave my key in the kitchen drawer."

"I'm not."

"I won't."

"Parker, honey you have until the count of ten." It sounds like Harper is next to my bed.

"Leave me alone. Please." I don't want to get out of my bed, and I don't want to face them. It's better in here.

"One…two…three…"

I feel a cool breeze come from the foot of the bed.

"Four…five…six…"

I hear giggling. *What are they about to do?*

"Seven…eight…nine…"

I know it's all nine of them as they count in unison.

"Ten!"

The cover pulls back, and I'm doused in ice cold water and sunlight.

"I'm going to kill y'all." I throw my hands around like I'm drowning. "And you got ice in my bed."

"Get up! We have more." Ryann is standing with an empty bucket in her hand, and Alex has the second bucket ready. I glare from Charlee to Jordan. My guys surround my bed, and they don't look happy.

"Fine. I'm up." I flick back the wet covers walking to the bathroom.

"Take a shower and get dressed." Hunter shoves a hanger in my direction.

"You have thirty minutes." Charlee tosses over her shoulder as they leave me alone.

"I hate y'all," I yell still in shock looking down at my pajamas plastered to my body.

"Love you too. Nine minutes Parker, we have a flight to catch."

HARPER SECURED a private jet from the fleet owned by her husband, Liam. And I sit in an uncomfortable silence with my best friends.

"Where are we going?"

They exchange glances, and Harper turns in my direction.

"New York."

"Why are we dressed in our business suits?"

"Because we have a client to secure, and you're up," Hunter says.

We sort of have uniforms when it's time to call in the big guns. All ten of us dressed in our Men in Black suits —dubbed GIB, *Guys in Black*. I think Hunter does it for dramatic effect. Ten beautiful black women strolling into a conference room like the bosses we are.

I honestly love to see the awe in the faces of anyone blessed to see the sight and tell the tale. But today, I'm nowhere near boss status. Because my heart is broken.

"Why am I up? I'm working on the building. It should be Ryann or Chase, anyone but me."

"You're up because we're headed to Wine & Dine Delivery."

The air leaves my lungs. "I can't."

"You can't or you won't?"

I don't know who said it and I don't care. "Both. I can't look him in the eyes after what happened."

"What happened?"

"Which part?" I brush away my tears.

"All of it Parker. We're your sisters. Tell us something because crawling in a hole away from the world is not the answer." Jordan holds my hand.

"I messed up. He wanted me to move to New York, and I refused."

"What do you want? We had a one o'clock appointment at his office."

"I want him back. But what if he refuses to see us?"

"Refuse?" Charlee pops her mouth. "All this fineness?"

"Why Lord…" I throw my head back, laughing.

"You don't have to ask the Lord for the answer to that. I got your answer." She scoots to the edge of her seat. "It's because I bring the average up."

We laugh so hard I swear the plane shakes. They say laughter is good for the soul. These women are good for me, and now I have to find a way to get my man back.

"We have an hour to create a plan. You're the lead guy on this one Parker. What are you going to do?"

"The question is, can I manage my workload from New York?" I glance over at Hunter.

"I don't see why not. Charlee and Taylor worked from California."

"We could see it as an opportunity to expand, as well," Chase adds. "Many of the brands we interact with have offices in New York."

I nod.

"What about your real estate company?"

"I can handle my exclusive properties, and I have my parents. It won't be easy, but it's not impossible. I can't believe I really considering this. I can't leave you guys."

"Who said anything about leaving? Besides, can you imagine the GIB in NYC?" Charlee snaps.

We slap fives, and my heart is happy and heavy. But I'm willing to do what I have to.

"READY?"

We are in the lobby of Wine & Dine Delivery. Our

plan is solid, and thank goodness we have the element of surprise on our side. Hunter managed to get us on his calendar.

My guys look amazing. I run to the bathroom for one last pep talk. I stand in the mirror, adjusting my glasses. I add a coat of ruby red lipstick because I need to wow him.

I step out ready to close the biggest deal of my life.

My guys, my sisters cross the lobby standing at my back. We load the elevator, and the moment the doors close, I face them.

Hunter, Harper, Charlee, Chase, Taylor, Payton, Alex, Ryann, and Jordan are dressed to kill, all in black. I can't ask for better friends. *I'm a blessed.*

"I don't know what I'd do without each of you. Thank you, and I love you all."

We have a group hug and take a minute to ensure we're all ready.

"The GIB is about to kill it," Alex says.

"We need to invest in a Beyoncé fan because they have *never* been blessed like this." Our laughter fills the elevator, and the ding the doors open.

"Guys, we're up."

CHAPTER 12

"Max, you're needed in the conference room."

I glance at the intercom. "When?"

"Immediately."

"Thanks, Grace." I sit aside the contracts I'm reviewing. I walk past her desk and ask, "Who am I meeting with?"

She scans her notes, "Darius Grant."

"Oh, that's a nice surprise. Show him in when you're ready."

My life has moved nonstop since we started moving Wine & Dine Delivery into Texas. It's been a much-needed distraction. But not enough for me to stop calling Darius in Austin to check on Parker. Now, I can ask about her in person.

I walk down the hall and enter the conference room. The other executives take their seats.

"Is he supposed to pitch?"

Grace looks over her glasses with a noncommittal shrug. I open my mouth to ask more questions when I hear the *click-clack* of heels coming towards us. I glance around the frame of the doorway, and I see them heading in my direction. Amore mio is leading her group of guys, and I pull out my phone to snap a picture.

Her hair is pulled up in the messy bun I like. The red lipstick on her has me ready to kiss her soft lips. But it's when our eyes meet that I know I'll do anything for her. Even moving back to Texas.

The guys stand in the doorway of the conference room. I hear several *hot damn*s around the room, and I don't blame them. I stand locking eyes with Parker.

"Good afternoon Mr. Bradley."

"Same to you, Miss Hamilton." She flashes me her killer smile.

"Whatever you want, my answer is yes." The room of executives laugh. "All kidding aside, the floor is yours, Miss Hamilton."

"Don't mind if I do."

CHAPTER 13

*T*ake a deep breath, thrilled that we closed the deal. The guys head out to grab lunch and give me a moment alone with Parker.

I remove my jacket removing a small box from my pocket.

"That was impressive."

I laugh. "How are you?"

"Better now. Get over here."

I walk over and let him hold me. I inhale, and I know wherever we are, he is home for me. My mother's words surface, and I truly understand. Max is a man worth leading, and it's time I tell him so.

"Got a second?"

"Step into my office."

I can't contain my nervous laugh. The Freedom Tour seems like a lifetime ago. I'm a different woman, and I'm willing to take a chance on love and him.

"I let my fears ruin our moment. You have every right to leave because I wasn't ready yet."

"And what's different now?"

He holds my trembling hands, and I clear my throat. I thought about this question for most of the flight here, and all the words seem to disappear until he smiles.

"I'm different. You asked what my dreams and passions are. I had a vague idea, but I know I want to spend the rest of my life with you. I know I want to grow old and raise my family on Texas soil. I know I want to build a legacy for our family like my parents did for me. But what I realized recently, I'm willing to change it all to have you."

His hands cup my face, and his mouth covers mine. "I love you, Parker. God, I love you."

"I love you too." I pull back and look into his amazing brown eyes. "I'm sorry, and I know you gave me a second chance. But if you can find it in your heart to give me a third, you won't regret it."

"Does this mean you'll consider moving to New York?"

"Yes."

"Yes?" The surprise on his face makes me laugh.

"Yes, Max." He pulls me close, and my heart pounds with his nearness. "I have one more request."

"Anything, amore mio."

"What does that mean? I know *tesoro mio* means my treasure."

"*Amore mio* means my heart."

The tears flow, and I hope I don't have makeup all over my best black suit. "That's sort of the perfect opening to my next request."

He stands closing his office door, he shakes the handle to ensure its locked.

"What's your request?"

I pull out a little black box. "Will you marry me?"

I CAN'T BELIEVE the day I've had. I pull Parker to her feet and lead her to my private elevator. The doors close behind us, and I remove her jacket, unbutton her blouse, and I remove the hair tie from her bun.

Her steamy eyes hold mine, and I can't wait to make love to her.

The doors open to my place, and I pull her inside. We don't talk or stop until I sit on the edge of the bed to unbutton her pants. I let my fingers caress her legs all the way down. She steps out, and I thank her.

My lips brush over hers as I remove her bra, telling her all the ways I intend to love her when I stand and kiss her. I walked away, and the gut-wrenching pain I endured was enough for me to stop trying to change Parker and love her.

I lower her to the bed, ready to feast on her sweet body, but first I undress.

"Are you still on the pill?"

"Yes." The heat in her eyes makes my shit rock hard.

"Have you been with anyone else?"

"No tesoro mio, all I want is you."

I crawl up the bed, positioning myself before slowly filling her. Her moans of pleasure drive my speed and my need to make her mine once and for all.

I tell her. Claiming her body, claiming her heart.

"This love is special Parker."

"I know Max."

We move as one whispering words of forever until her declaration of love settles in my soul. I buckle my release moments after she screams my name, and everything in my world is right again.

I fall back gasping for air.

"Is that a yes, Max?" I glance over at her then over at my night stand. I open the drawer and pull out my own jewelry box.

"Will you marry me?" This was the sign I needed that I'm not in this love alone.

"Yes!" She kisses all over my face before lowering her body onto mine.

"Big wedding or a little wedding?" She rocks her hips, and I can't believe she's ready to go again.

"Little."

I take a sweet nipple into my mouth. "How many kids do you want?"

"At least three," she moans, her head falling back.

"Pets?"

"Uh-huh." I know the end is near by her grip on my shoulders. "Long or short engagement?"

"Short."

"Austin or New York?"

"Austin." Her eyes drop to mine, and they fill with tears.

"Really, Max?"

"Really love." I watch ecstasy dance across her face before I cradle her to my heart.

"I'm staying here until you're ready to move back." Her eyes struggle to remain open then she's out, and I'm in heaven, certain that loving her is what I was born to do.

Six months later...

I can't believe this is our house. I kick the boxes aside. The house where we first reconnected is now our first home together.

"Parker, the bus is pulling up."

I run to the door. I open it wide, "Are y'all ready to party?"

"Lies...all lies. I can see the boxes over your shoulder." Charlee says, leaning in for a sideways hug. "Check out Ryann's date."

I glance over her shoulder. I hug all the guys until Ryann brings up the rear. "I'd like to introduce you to Xavier."

"Nice to meet you." I shake his hand.

"Same to you."

Max calls the men inside. The guys stand around,

waiting for Ryann to explain. I look at Charlee ready for her to make a dive in on this one and apparently, I'm not the only one, as we steal quick glances her way.

"What?" Ryann laughs. "He's a guy I met a few weeks ago."

"How old is he?"

"Old enough."

"Old enough to do what, buy a damn drink?" Charlee rests a hand on her lower back. We laugh.

"Old enough for me to enjoy and that's all you need to know. Nosey."

She sashays inside, and I share a shrug with Harper.

"Go on then Stella. Get your groove on." Charlee's fake Jamaican accent is awful, and we all laugh heading into the house.

We stop in the living room, and I see Max across the room. He mouths, *Love you*. I blow a kiss.

"Girl stop staring into space and come help. You know I'm allergic to boxes." Charlee yells.

Yeah, I'm a special woman with a beautiful life. I can't believe how much my life has changed. I work from home most days, and Platinum Prestige is skyrocketing.

Plus, I'm married to an amazing man. I can't wait to tell him that our little family of two will be three soon. I press play on the music and the like that the party begins.

I watch Ryann rock her hips dancing with your man and I ain't mad at her. I guess love is in the air again.

～

THANK you for reading **SPECIAL LOVE**. Parker and Max found their happily ever after. Keep reading and meet Ryann and Xavier in *Absolute Love*.

I'm sitting in a luncheon and my boss announces that I'm the first female African American partner under the age of thirty in the history of the firm.

I'm Ryann Gibson. I practice corporate law by day and hang with my guys by night, as a partner of Platinum Prestige. My bank account is fat, my house is laid, but my bed is cold and empty.

Dating at this stage of my life mirrors the setup of a bad joke. What do you get when you…fill in the blank? Meet an old guy? Meet a broke guy? Meet a young guy?

When Xavier, our waiter, asks me out I wait for the rest of the joke. Because he has three strikes against him.

He's young, cocky, and he just quit his job. His confidence intrigues me and our instant attraction has me saying yes when I should say no.

Little do I know, I'm signing up for the ride of my life. Nor how this one concession sets my cold bed ablaze and all work, no play becomes all night, all day.

But when the smoke clears, can two people so different find love?

One-click ABSOLUTE LOVE now!

AUTHOR'S NOTE

I said YES to a holiday romance writing project in 2019.

Ten authors. Ten holidays. Ten steamy romances. And we've all said yes to taking this journey together.

My ten stories are novella length. I think they're great for an evening of reading with your favorite glass of wine or tea. :) And I had the group of guys to make this series happen.

Then struts in Hunter and her squad, her guys. They came to me years ago. I love a good millionaire or billionaire romance like the next woman. But a few of my readers emailed me asking about a female millionaire. I thought why settle for one if I can write ten. **insert evil laugh**

I hope you enjoyed book one with Harper and Liam. Will you join me for the rest of the year as they build Platinum Prestige—one fly millionaire woman and hot guy at a time?

Don't miss a single release. Join my newsletter at **http://www.janesedixon.com/subscribe** to get updates and reader specials FIRST.

In closing, please leave a review. It helps others find my work and it keeps the lights on, if you know what I mean. ;)

I'll "see" you all soon.

Happy Reading,
Ja'Nese Dixon
www.janesedixon.com

P.S. Again, there are more Steamy Sensations Holiday Love stories available now. See them all on my website: http://www.janesedixon.com/steamy-sensations.

LEAVE A REVIEW

Did you enjoy *Chosen Love*?

Please leave a book review **HERE**. Reviews are extremely important and it helps me continue sharing my books with fellow readers.

JOIN MY NEWSLETTER

Be the FIRST to know!

Consider joining my newsletter? http://www. janesedixon.com/subscribe Be the first to know about releases and specials. You can unsubscribe anytime.

BOOK 1

It's Valentine's Day.

I run to my favorite bar determined to figure out how I managed to lose my man and my inheritance in one night. The man is replaceable, but my monthly stipend is not.

I'm Hunter Preston. My friends call me Jo and I'm the only child to a media mogul. I was traveling the world, living my best life, until Daddy dropped a million-dollar bomb, annihilating my boujee world.

Double or nothing.

He gave me thirty days to pitch a million dollar business concept, or I can say goodbye to my trust fund.

So, here I am with my girls, trying to get more than selfie advice, when Ben, the sexy bartender—who either abhors me or he's immune to my flirting—offers to help write the business plan under one condition. He wants $50,000.

$50k to get $1 mil sounds reasonable until I remember how hot he is and how off-limits he is and how he wants nothing to do with a woman like me.

I'm screwed, pass me another drink.

**Get Your Copy on Amazon
or Read in Kindle Unlimited!**

Read an excerpt on www.janesedixon.com.

BOOK 2

It's St. Patrick's Day.

The day is really not important, at least that's what I thought. I dress to impress, ready to secure my first contract as a partner with Platinum Prestige.

Simple, right? No, I wish.

I'm Harper Price. I've joined my best friends in starting an elite concierge service and I'm up. My sole task is to lease an airplane from Liam.

I walk in, he proposes, I walk out.

Apparently, his billionaire have gone to his head and now the sexy, arrogant menace won't leave me alone. His head is hard as a brick. (Take that any way you want.) And he refuses to accept "no" in any language. But I'm done with love.

No more.

Nada.

No mas.

Yet secretly, I'm scribbling my first name with his last name. Then he whispers, "Live a little Harper." And his money green eyes shine like dollars signs as he throws an unexpected curve ball. He'll grant three wishes, when…not if…I say yes.

Does having the most eligible rich bachelor begging to put a ring on it make me lucky? Hell no!

Not when my heart is screaming leap, my head is screaming caution, and my panties are.…

Oh hell, this is a f'in plane crash waiting to happen.

What is a woman to do?

Get Your Copy on Amazon
or Read in Kindle Unlimited!

Read an excerpt on www.janesedixon.com.

BOOK 6

Can two people so different find love?

I'm sitting in a luncheon and my boss announces that I'm the first female African American partner under the age of thirty in the history of the firm.

I'm Ryann Gibson. I practice corporate law by day and hang with my guys by night, as a partner of Platinum Prestige. My bank account is fat, my house is laid, but my bed is cold and empty.

Dating at this stage of my life mirrors the setup of a bad joke. What do you get when you…fill in the blank? Meet an old guy? Meet a broke guy? Meet a young guy?

When Xavier, our waiter, asks me out I wait for the rest of the joke. Because he has three strikes against him.

He's young, cocky, and he just quit his job. His confidence intrigues me and our instant attraction has me saying yes when I should say no.

Little do I know, I'm signing up for the ride of my life. Nor how this one concession sets my cold bed ablaze and all work, no play becomes all night, all day.

But when the smoke clears, can two people so different find love?

PreOrder YOUR Copy!

Millions of adoring fans dream of having one night with him, but only she has access to his heart.

Born with three commas in his bank account and melodies in his veins, Marques Carter is the rising prince of R&B. But not even his family name can guarantees success.

Brione Allen is a smart woman that made a dumb decision: trusting the wrong man. He blackmailed her family and now she's bound by a debt they knew she couldn't pay.

A chance meeting at his concert leads to an encrypted proposal: One week, one hundred thousand dollars, one incriminating secret. But when extortion and family ties expose them to the worst of the limelight, which secrets will they keep…and which will threaten their small light of hope?

**Get Your Copy on Amazon
or Read in Kindle Unlimited!**

CHAPTER 1

*T*he same time every week for three years and the call got no easier. Brione Allen sat on the couch and blew out a deep breath. Dial the number. Ask for Kayla. But the knot in her stomach told the utter truth. Nothing about this was easy for her.

She tapped the numbers by memory, adding it to her favorites was something she couldn't stomach, not after all they'd done to her.

"Hello."

"Good evening Mrs. Bradley is Kayla around?" She stopped asking to speak with her hoping to gain a sense of control in the situation, but they held her captive with a vice grip on her heart.

"Hello to you too Brione." Her dusty voice held an air of censorship. "I'll call for her."

Kayla had a nanny, private school, and just about everything a little girl could want.

"Brione." She cringed at hearing his voice.

"Stewart, I was holding for Kayla."

"She'll have to call you back."

"But today is my—"

"Talk to you later."

The line disconnected and Brione screamed. No one heard her, and no one cared. Alone in her fancy plush prison, she'd gladly trade for their freedom.

She fell back on the couch and stared at the ceiling fan and her cellphone rang. She popped up anticipating the sweet sound of Kayla's voice. But the screen displayed another welcomed caller.

"Eliana Marshall. To what do I owe this honor?" Laughter flowed through the phone, Eliana was the only person she let close. The only person she trusted. The only person who knew the truth.

"Let's see…I'm your best friend. So I need no reason to call other than to hear your wonderful voice." Brione smiled. "Second, I'm flying into town, and I refuse any excuse you make for not seeing me."

Brione gripped the phone to her ear as she toyed with the hem of her blouse. She'd rushed home from work for nothing.

"I apologized a million times. But you plan to milk it dry," she joked pulling her stocking covered feet beneath her body and relaxed.

"I plan to milk it until it turns to powder if that will get your butt out of that condo. I will *not* take no for an answer."

"Milk it dry *and* add in a level of guilt to the recipe."

"You got it." They laughed. "How are you?"

"I've been better." Brione looked around the room, furnished with the finest, reeking of their wealth. "You're heading here for the weekend?"

"No, I'm heading back indefinitely. Bruce and his wife are expecting twins, and they're keeping a close watch on her. We're planning to hang out in Houston until the babies arrive. Her doctor and family are all there. So, it could be a couple of months or longer."

"Yay!" Brione sat up, excited. "It will be nice to have you in town for a while."

"Just know I plan to pop up on your doorstep and drag you to a party or two while I'm there." Brione shook her head knowing they would have a battle ahead.

"How are you enjoying your job?"

Brione listened as Eliana shared her love of working for Bruce Daniels. She bounced around from Atlanta to Houston and back as his assistant.

"I can't believe the luck I've had with getting this job. It is stressful but fun. I'll be assisting Marques for a while too."

"Who is that?" The name sounded familiar, in a fuzzy, vague way.

"What rock do you live under?"

"The law school rock." She snickered. "I don't have time for anything but class and studying. Well, that and my side gig."

"Side gig?"

"Eliana, who is Marques?"

"Oh, yeah. How do you *not* know who he is?" Her amazement was evident by the squeak in her voice. "He's a caramel dipped...tall, muscled...*god* in living color."

Brione lifted a brow at Eliana's description. "All that?"

"Yes, he's the epitome of sexy. Too bad he's my boss." She let out a sigh. "Anyway, he's an R&B singer from Atlanta. I guess you wouldn't know him since he's more underground." She was all business. "He is the flagship artist of Rockstar Entertainment. We're preparing to release an EP then his debut album."

Brione tried to picture this caramel sexy god. Her failed attempt morphed into her last dalliance that turned her life upside down, inside out, and left Brione estranged from her family.

"That sounds like a lot of work." Brione didn't listen to the radio and rarely watched TV. Her sights were set on securing an associate's position with a major law firm. Fun took a backseat.

"It is, which is part of the reason for my call." Eliana said.

"Oh, it wasn't just to hear my wonderful voice?"

"Of course."

"Yeah, yeah, yeah. Spill it, Honey." Brione walked to the kitchen and opened the freezer, pushing around the contents until she found the frozen lasagna.

"Do you still help with events?"

"Yes, what's up?" She peeled back the corner of the lid

and popped the plastic bowl into the microwave. Then she leaned a hip against the counter.

"Bruce's anticipated maternity leave and Marques' EP has opened a lot of doors for me. They've asked me to oversee the launch with hopes of promoting me to A&R."

"Congrats!"

"Thanks, but hold it for now. I still need to get through this project."

"So, basically it's an interview."

"Exactly."

"How can I help?" Brione dropped her head and chuckled at the faint sounds of Eliana's clapping. Eliana could make it happen without her, but Brione wanted to see her friend succeed. "I didn't say yes yet."

"But you will." Eliana blew a kiss through the phone. "I want to host a release party in Houston, and I'd love to bring you in. It pays good, and I'm almost certain I can get you the gig."

"Really? But I've never done a music event."

"Don't worry about that. Your work is impeccable, you're organized, timely, and you work well under extreme pressure. Are you free Saturday?"

"Yes, how about ten?"

"That's perfect. Get together your portfolio and let's meet at the cafe on Saturday. I'll try to get either Bruce or Marques there too. That way I can cross two tasks off my list at once."

"I like the sound of that."

"You would, Miss Planner Chic. I maintain, where you thrive. One day, I'll grow up to be just like you."

Brione shook her head as if Eliana could see her. "No, ma'am. Grow up to be like you, and you'll be just fine."

"The thought of peanut butter and honey back in business is enticing don't you think."

"Houston ain't ready for us," Brione added.

Eliana's robust laughter rang through the phone. "Girl, if only they knew! And for totally selfish reasons, it would be a lifesaver to have your help *and* get to spend time with you without you skipping out on me."

They haven't seen each other in years, for one reason or another. But Brione missed her too. "I got you. When we're done, they're going to beg you to take that position. And I'll be there at 9:45 ready to rock n' roll."

"Awesome. I'll text you if anything changes. I gotta go, we're about to land." Eliana said.

"Be safe." The microwave beeped.

"I will. Love you Peanut Butter." Eliana giggled.

"Love you too Honey." They disconnected, Brione stood staring at the phone for a minute considering their long friendship.

Eliana was her roommate in college, their running nicknames came when all they could afford was Ramen noodles, and peanut butter and jelly, except Eliana, liked hers with honey or syrup.

Music was Eliana's passion like organizing events was Brione's. However, she knew her love of centerpieces and tulle could not lead to her desired destination.

Brione gathered her hot food from the microwave and walked to the dining room, she turned into an office. She stared at the stack of textbooks. She entered law school for two reasons: money and time. The family connections between the Bradleys and her parents guaranteed her seat. But her high GPA landed her a full ride.

She cleared a space for her bowl, tonight she'd study and tomorrow she'd order pizza and work on her portfolio. She lowered into the chair in front of her laptop, placing her food aside. She opened the oversized law book and turned to the cases she needed to read and analyze for class tomorrow.

She leaned over the keyboard and forked a chunk of lasagna, she cradled her hand beneath it to keep the sauce from dripping onto her expensive textbooks. She popped it into her mouth and did a chair dance as the ricotta cheese and Italian sausage made her taste buds happy, momentarily overlooking that it almost burnt her tongue. She pushed the bowl back to let it cool and read the first legal case when her phone rang again. The little face on the screen made her heart race with joy.

"Hello, Sweet Pea." Her voice trembled, she took a deep breath.

"Hi!" Brione could envision her chubby cheeks, full eye lashes, and radiant smile.

"I think this is the best surprise I've had all day." Her giggle warmed Brione's heart. "How was school today?"

Kayla talked about crayons and finger painting. Her

new best friend and a boy pulling her pigtails. All the things Brione had to experience by phone and not in person. And as soon as the call started it ended, sending exaggerated kisses through the phone to the tune of Kayla's sweet laughter with promises of talking with her again on Saturday.

Life wasn't fair. That was too tall of an order.

Brione used the fork to cut into the cooler lasagna. She had stopped crying about it and questioning why long ago, instead she dealt with it, taking blow by blow and somehow managing to bounce back. But tonight she wanted to sit in it. From the sting of the scheduled phone calls to Stewart consistently dangling their freedom like cheese enticing a rat, reminding herself that she had a plan. This ache in her chest was only temporary.

One day she and Kayla would live under the same roof. Holding on to this goal kept her in one piece.

Kayla motivated Brione to work hard and she vowed not to repeat the same mistake twice. Men like the dreamy caramel sex god Eliana drooled over were bad news. Stewart was one of them. He walked into a room and every woman—married, single, it didn't matter—wanted him. She'd thought herself lucky.

Brione snickered at her foolish youth. None of them cared about what she wanted in life. Her goals. Her desires. To the Bradleys, her parents, Stewart, she was their pawn, their minion, their tool. *So they thought.*

She couldn't afford to crack. She ate the rest of her

dinner, deciding to study first then get her portfolio together for her meeting with Eliana.

To get Kayla back, she needed money and landing the job with Eliana to organize Marques' event could be the break she'd prayed for.

CHAPTER 2

*W*alking into Coffee Confessions had a ring of a homecoming for Marques Carter. He had spent many days hanging around waiting on Bruce to finish a shift before they went to the studio. Houston saved him and got his life back on course. Now that he was back, he hoped lightning would strike again for them.

He pulled the baseball cap lower to disguise himself. The release of his first official video last week gave him more than his usual double takes. In Atlanta, he couldn't go anywhere without people recognizing him, here offered a reprieve. But he didn't want to take any chances, welcoming the way people bumped right past him. It added another reason he loved being back in Houston.

Marques arrived early to meet with Bruce. He scanned the room, spotting a few empty tables and made his way to the line. He lifted his head to read the menu when he felt a soft bump behind him. He turned around and had to glance down at a petite woman.

"Excuse me." She held up a hand then reached out to stabilize a mug rocking back and forth on the shelf. "I was trying to miss the stroller and then the display and…" Her voice stalled as she finally looked up at him. Her lips parted in surprise. "Huh, sorry."

He chuckled. "I think I'll live."

She nodded without speaking as their gazes held. Marques let his eyes survey her light brown skin paired with jet black hair. It was curled softly brushing the sides of her face in a chic bob. Her heart-shaped face and doe eyes held curiosity as her full lashes brushed her high cheekbones with each exaggerated blink behind black frames. But when he zeroed in on her full lips coated with a hint of gloss, her tongue darted out and a groan reached his ears. He didn't know if it came from him or her.

"Andrew Carter." Using his legal name seemed appropriate as he extended a hand ready to see if her skin was as soft as it appeared.

"Brione Allen." Her smooth husky tone reminded him of a midnight radio jockey. The type of voice that held intrigue, mystery, and allure.

She accepted his hand and lightning passed from her touch through his body. *Damn.* Her eyes flashed to meet his as his heart rate tripled. He studied her thoughtfully, appreciating the heat lingering in the depths of her brown eyes.

"Welcome to Coffee Confessions, give in to your guilty pleasure. How can I be of service?" The barista behind the counter asked and Marques was at a loss for words. He still held her delicate hand in his thinking Miss Brione Allen was a guilty pleasure he'd gladly give in to. But judging by the penetrating stare she gave him as she snatched her hand away from his, he doubted she was on the menu.

"I'm sorry, I need a moment to review the menu. Brione after you." He extended his hand towards the counter and she stepped forward. She appeared as surprised as he was. The chemistry between them was as real as the nose on his face.

"Huh, sure." She stepped to the counter and tossed her purse on her shoulder like a barrier between them. *No, baby girl, that purse ain't gonna save you.*

She started to order and the sounds of the room faded into oblivion as Marques scanned the length of her body, the curve of her backside, and...

"And for you sir?" The barista wiggled his eyebrows. Heat rose to Marques' face, *caught.* But her hips were too tempting to ignore in pants that left no curve to the imagination.

"Our order is not tog—"

"Make it two of what she's having." He passed his credit card and turned back to Brione.

"That's not necessary."

"You're welcome," he teased, her expression much too severe for him.

Her eyes softened, "Thank you."

Brione stepped to the side and waited as Marques collected his receipt. They stood in heated silence both snagging discreet glances at the other waiting for their coffee. He had no clue what she ordered, thankfully he wasn't allergic to anything.

His senses were ablaze with her nearness. The closest comparison would be the moment he completed a new song. It gave the dueling emotions of exhilaration and exhaustion simultaneously.

"Are you off to work today?" He noticed the button up blouse and dress slacks.

"No, I'm meeting a friend. And you?"

"Business." She scanned his body in a sweeping motion. He wore a baseball cap with jeans and shirt. His goal was to blend in with the good people of Houston. He wished now that he'd given it more thought. Her mouth took on an unpleasant twist. "What you don't approve of my casual attire?"

"Oh no. I think it must be nice."

He searched her eyes and wished he could read her mind. The barista called his name for the order. Marques passed a cup to her and grabbed his own. The place was filling up quickly. He snagged a table and pulled out a chair for her.

"Join me while you wait." She hesitated. "Please." Brione slowly lowered to the chair. The floral scent of her perfume couldn't compete with the aroma of the coffee beans but it was a soft statement of her presence in the busy cafe.

Marques sat across from her finding it hard to contain the odd sensation in the pit of his stomach. He took a drink of the hot coffee to distract himself. The taste of caramel and whipped cream warmed his mouth. "This is delicious. What is it?"

"A custom drink. It's my favorite." She lifted the cup to her mouth and took a sip too. Remnants of her gloss left on the white lid.

"I'll have to get this again." He grabbed his phone and snapped a picture of the sleeve. "So Brione tell me, are you from Houston?"

She sat her cup on the table, pulling closer. Their knees brushed, her eyes widened. "No."

He waited for her to continue, she crossed her hands over the table. "Are you always this talkative?"

Her husky laughter rippled through the air. "No, it takes me a minute to warm up to people."

He nodded. Brione dropped her hands to her lap, "What about you? Are you from here?"

"No, I'm from Georgia."

"You said you're here on business. What type of business are you in?"

"I'm in a family business. I'm taking a little time off before we enter a busy season." It was obvious she didn't recognize him. It made him relax, he didn't feel "on."

"Do you travel often?" She asked.

"Not as often as I'd like."

"So you enjoy traveling?"

He nodded, "I do. It is a love of mine, I acquired it as a child. I traveled a lot with my parents." He took a drink of his coffee. He joined his father on many tours over the years. "The food, architecture, music, museums, I love all of it."

"Where all have you visited?" The warmth of her smile echoed in her voice.

He crossed his arms over his chest and extended his legs. "I visited, at last count, 40 or so of the great states of America. I've hit the tourist spots. Australia, Canada, South Africa, Rome, London, Egypt, I love it there too. Dubai, New Zealand, India, China, Morocco, Italy, Bali. There are more but you put me on the spot."

"Tell me about your favorite place." She leaned over the table and rested her chin in her hand. Her eyes bright and inquisitive.

"Uh…" her smile made it hard to think straight, he searched his mind, "I can't pick just one. My most recent trip was to Bora Bora."

"That place is on my wish list." A smile danced on her lips, heat coursed through his veins. *Get a grip!*

"Put a star by it. It is a place you'll never forget. The warmth of the water. Its vibrant turquoise color. There's something magical and healing about the island."

Her expression stilled and grew serious.

"Add this one to your wish list too." He wanted to see her smile again. "Torres del Paine National Park."

The spark returned. "Where is that?"

Marques leaned forward enjoying the light in her eyes. "It's in Chile. There's more sheep than people but the valleys are the most vibrant green and the sky the bluest blue you'll ever see. There is a small window when the weather is appropriate but it is worth it." He winked and something told him she mentally noted every word.

He wondered what she was thinking as she dropped her head, brushing her hair behind her ears. Her phone buzzed against the table and Brione glanced down at the screen.

"That's my friend." She held up her phone and finished her coffee. "We have to reschedule."

She stood from the table and leaned over to toss the empty cup in the trash.

"Would you like another?"

"No, I have studying to do."

"Studying?" He hoped to prolong her departure.

"I'm a law student." The glimmer in her eyes dulled.

"If I remember correctly there are three of them here."

"You are absolutely correct." She placed her purse on her shoulder and picked up a black portfolio. He missed that earlier.

"Would you like to grab lunch or something?"

"I really need to go." She shook her head and glanced at her phone. "Thank you for the coffee and the conversation." An easy smiled played at the corners of her mouth.

"No, thank you for this wonderful concoction." He held up the cup shaking it.

"You're welcome. Have a nice day." She turned to leave and he reached for her arm.

"Take my number. I'm in town for a couple weeks. I *really* would like to see you again."

"I don't have time. I—"

"Take it…just in case. Pass me your phone and I'll enter it."

She searched his eyes for so long he thought she'd say no again.

"Okay." She hesitantly passed her unlocked phone, holding the top with the tip of her fingers, as if trying to avoid his touch.

He entered his personal cellphone number and placed the phone in her open palm. "I'll talk with you soon."

CHAPTER 3

*B*rione sat to study for finals, she had two weeks left before summer break. But his voice, his smile barraged her. "Study Bri!"

Thoughts of coffee with Andrew had her head in the clouds. The way his head fell back when he laughed. The twinkle in his eyes when he teased her. It was a chasm in time that passed too fast, she wanted more.

Closing her eyes she estimated his height was close to six feet, the outlines of his shoulders strained against the fabric of his shirt. He stood before her with his hands shoved in his pockets and a killer smile wide with perfect white teeth. His classically handsome features made him beautiful for a man.

People passed their table slowing to gawk at him, not once did he look away or acknowledge their presence. She wondered what his hair looked like beneath the cap but figured it really didn't matter. The man could be bald and she was sure she'd find him absolutely breathtaking —star quality.

Brione shook her head trying to rattle the images of him from her memories. But it proved impossible.

She tried reading the case at least ten times with no luck. But his soft encouragement, add this one to your wish list, rendered it impossible. Adding him to her list sound better. *Forget it.*

She opened her laptop and clicked on an internet browser. She typed in, Torres del Paine National Park and pressed enter. The results populated, her inner child didn't know where to start. She squealed stomping her feet beneath the table to release the energy. Pictures, she'd start there.

Brione clicked on "Images." The pictures before her eyes made her lean into the monitor. There were mountains, valleys, glaciers, snow, a winter heaven. What had he done during his visit? Did he hike? Was he alone? Was it as cold as it appeared?

She grabbed her phone and went back to his contact. And she noticed the note, Call me and let's have dinner sometime. She had stared at it for most of her *non-effective* study time.

She could send a text.

Her fingers hovered over the screen. No. She shook her head, and then what? He'd text her back and want to talk on the phone. She put the phone back on the table. Music. That would help.

She stood and turned on the wireless speaker,

stopping by the kitchen for some water. Back at the coffee table, she sat in front of her textbook. She untwisted the top off the plastic bottle and took a cool drink. She scanned her phone for some music, pressed play and turned back to the case.

Brione read through several immigration cases for class. Her doorbell rang and she glanced at the clock. She wasn't expecting anyone, she never had guests except... She stood up and walked to the door and glanced through the peephole. Her heart dropped to her feet. *What is he doing here?*

Stewart leaned into the doorbell. *Ding dong. Ding dong. Ding dong.*

"I know you're there. Open up and stop staring at me through the peephole."

Brione jerked back, placing her back against the door. She cracked her knuckles and exhaled a shaky breath. Her palms sweaty, she looked down at her t-shirt and leggings. Her clothes didn't matter. But she felt more in control in a suit. Less like the young woman that fell for his smile and honey-laced words only to get stung by a wasp.

"You can do this Bri," she whispered running her wet hands down her pants. She clutched one hand in the other to still her shaking limbs. "This is your space. You are in control."

Ding dong. Ding dong. Ding dong.

"I'm not leaving." He stated.

She placed a hand on the handle and unlocked the

bolt. She peeked through the opening created by the chain. "What do you want?"

"I promise this is not the way you want to handle this situation." He leveled his deadly stare.

"I'm studying."

"I guess Kayla will call you next week then. Give you time to study." He stepped back never breaking eye contact with her. She unlatched the chain, stepping back as he strolled in like he owned the place.

Brione closed the door. Stewart was like the boogeyman. People refute its existence until it pops up under your bed.

He sat on the couch and leaned back. "Are you always this rude to your guests?" He stretched his arms across the cushions, obviously comfortable. "Can I get some water, sweet tea, a sandwich? Damn." He laughed at his own joke.

"You didn't drive to Houston for water or a sandwich. So stop with the dramatics. What do you want?"

"What I've always wanted, *you*."

Stewart Bradley knew how to pop up on her doorstep when she felt confident, when she finally decided to not let him push her around, then he emerged from the shadows to call her bluff.

"Have a seat? I won't bite."

The invisible shackles clanked around her ankles as she sat in the chair closest to the door. "What do you want Stewart?"

"How are you?" His eyes scanned her body. She

wrapped her arms protectively around her waist.

"I'm fine."

"When did you cut your hair and what's up with your clothes?"

"Stewart I'm studying." His mother was always dressed to perfection including a string of white pearls. He wanted a clone of Mrs. Bradley, the thought of her old sweats and short hair irking him brought a smile to her face. "And I like my bob."

"Is this how you're carrying yourself nowadays?"

"Is that why you visited? If so, we can end this conversation here and now." She swallowed hard.

"Don't let law school go to your head. This is still my show."

"Why don't you move on and let us move on too?"

"There is no *us* without me," he growled. "You got into law school because of me. You can't care for Kayla without a job. What about her education? Her tutors? Her nanny? And don't forget about your pops." His glare intimidating. "I will deliver his career in a wastebasket. Is that what you want? Do you want to ruin everyone's lives because of your selfishness?"

The boogeyman live and in living color. Panic was rioting inside her gnawing away at her confidence. Gnawing away at her plans and dousing her hope.

She once trusted this man and thought he loved her. That was the face of love. It was laughable. Her tongue felt thick and her nerves made it hard to form a coherent thought. She was tired of him pushing her around.

Don't let him push you around. Brione couldn't trust that voice, hadn't she invited him into her life in the first place. She dropped her head, stirring uneasily in the chair, hoping to hide the shame from his probing eyes. It was the cost of trusting an untrustworthy person. A person who valued self-ambition and greed over people. *How had I missed it?*

"Are you done playing with me?" His nostrils flared with fury.

She nodded, fear splintered her heart.

"Good." The storm clouds left his eyes. "Mom wants us to set a date."

She squeezed her eyes shut gripping the arms of the chair. "Stewart you don't want to marry me. We have nothing in common—"

"Nothing in common? We have *everything* in common. Let me shoot it to you straight. I want a date or so help me, Brione Allen, I'll bury you and your father's dreams of sitting in the Oval Office. And I'll ensure you never ever see our daughter again." He ground the words out through clenched teeth. "Understand?"

"Yes."

~

Continue Reading...

**Get Your Copy on Amazon
or Read in Kindle Unlimited!**

Ready for Love Series (Sweet Romance)

Caramel Surprise (Book 1)

Love's Hope (Book 2)

Hidden Desire (Book 3)

Ready for Love Boxed Set (Books 1 - 3)

Smith Pact Duo (Contemporary Romance)

Yuki's Luck (Book 1)

Tempting Asher (Book 2)

Smith Surprise (Book 3)

See all of my books on my website:

http://www.janesedixon.com/books.

HOLIDAY LOVE

10 Authors. 10 Holidays. 10 *Steamy Romances*.

Ten romance authors bring you a sexy story to fire up your holiday. Each author has their own series in 2019 with one thing in common - Holidays!

Check out all of the Steamy Sensations books HERE or my website janesedixon.com/steamy-sensations!

ABOUT THE AUTHOR

Ja'Nese Dixon pens tales of romance in several subgenres. But her favorites are the ones that manage to keep readers sitting on the edge of their seats lying to themselves about reading "just one more chapter".

Ja'Nese is an avid reader and coffee drinker, who also loves to run, cook, and craft. Her ultimate goal as a writer is to give you a little "staycation" with every story. And she aims to make this present story no exception. Sit back, grab a snack and enjoy.

Ja'Nese calls Houston home with her husband, three kiddos and a four-legged diva dog.

Visit her website at www.janesedixon.com if you enjoy romance, suspense and good stories.

Subscribe to Ja'Nese Newsletter "Reader's Staycation" for reader exclusives, regular giveaways and more.

Stay in Touch:
www.janesedixon.com
info@janesedixon.com

facebook.com/AuthorJaNeseDixon

twitter.com/janesedixon

instagram.com/authorjanesedixon

amazon.com/author/janesedixon

bookbub.com/authors/ja-nese-dixon

ABOUT THE PUBLISHER

Purpose Prevails Publishing
2231B Center St. STE 144
Deer Park, TX 77536
www.purposeprevailspublishing.com

www.ingramcontent.com/pod-product-compliance
Lightning Source LLC
Chambersburg PA
CBHW020139180626
46810CB00004B/1633